Three Friends

A CHARLOTTE ZOLOTOW BOOK

Three Friends
by Myron Levoy

1 8  1 7
——————— HARPER & ROW, PUBLISHERS ———————

Cambridge, Philadelphia, San Francisco, London, Mexico City, São Paulo, Sydney

——————— NEW YORK ———————

For Bea

Library of Congress Cataloging in Publication Data
Levoy, Myron.
    Three friends.

    "A Charlotte Zolotow book."
    Summary: Three very different high school classmates
find their friendship severely tested by the pressures
of growing up.
    [1. Individuality—Ficton.   2. Friendship—Fiction]
I. Title
PZ7.L5825Th 1984   [Fic]   83-47713
ISBN 0-06-023826-7
ISBN 0-06-023827-5 (lib. bdg.)

1

It was early May, and the time was drawing near for swimming at the lake. Joshua Freeman studied his body in the full-length mirror—the slender frame, the face with the large dark eyes, the dangling arms. Nothing seemed right. Nothing would ever be right. It didn't really matter. What girl would ever bother with him anyway, naked, clothed, or standing on his head? He would avoid the lake again this year.

"Joshua!" It was his mother's voice from downstairs. "Joshua, are you still asleep?"

He flexed his arms and saw the biceps slightly knot, but they were thin and stringy, without power. It was power that was missing, and coordination. He had tried desperately to play basketball and tennis, to learn to dive, but the simplest movements became awkward pantomimes as he struggled to make his body behave. When other boys dived off the dock at the lake, they would cut downward like thrown knives. Joshua had often watched them enviously.

He stared down at the dark curling hair. That wasn't right either, not enough, not thick and full. And the size. He had found averages in sex manuals in the bookstores, and he was below average. He'd taken the average of all the averages, but he was still below average. He would never ever have a girl friend, or get married, or anything, because it would be humiliating. They would laugh at him. Make jokes. Horrible.

"Joshy!" his mother called again.

"I'm still asleep!" he called back.

"Will you please come downstairs!"

"I can't right now! I'm in the middle of an important dream!" Yes. A nightmare, he thought. His body.

Sometimes he would talk to himself as if he were a psychologist, reassuring himself that things like those silly averages didn't matter at all. It helped, and he'd decided that if he ever changed his mind about chess as a career, he would be a psychologist and help others, the way the secret psychologist in him helped him. But he would never change his mind.

On his shelves were half a dozen paperbacks on psychology, but there were over forty books on chess overflowing into a pile on the floor. A book he'd been reading on Queen's Gambit openings lay on his bed; as he

2

searched for his underwear, he flipped through the book again.

Chess. It was there that the power in him lay, where the free leap into space could happen. In the intricate dance of chess, he knew he could be as graceful as any twisting, turning center slamming a ball down into the basket. Chess came first, even before school. Even before sleep.

At fourteen and a half, he'd almost achieved master rank. He was the highest-rated player within his age group in New Jersey, and sixth in the entire United States. Could he ever be first? It was so difficult. If only he had someone he could talk to about it. About everything. Everything! Even those ridiculous averages.

The only close friend he'd ever had was a fellow chess player, Bob Kim. They'd met at the Metropolitan Chess Club in New York City and had lived, breathed, and eaten chess together for almost two years. But Bob's father had changed jobs a year ago and moved to Los Angeles. Joshua and Bob still played chess by mail, but the close friendship had been demolished by distance.

"Joshua, don't make me have to come up!" his mother called. "I've had enough problems with your father this morning. Nobody listens to me in this house!" Oh, please, thought Joshua.

"I'm getting dressed!" he shouted toward the door.

He pulled on his briefs and checked himself in the mirror once more. The underwear was loose; if he jumped up and down, it would fall off. He jumped and the briefs slid down. He tossed the underwear into the wastebasket. "Parting is such sweet sorrow!" he called toward the basket with a bitter laugh, then remembered he had to read the fourth act of *Romeo and Juliet* for English, before Monday.

He took another pair of underwear from the drawer, then dressed quickly, trying not to notice himself in the mirror. But every article of clothing—the jeans, the shirt, even the socks—seemed large and shapeless. Worse, he, himself, was shapeless. And skinny. Juliet would have mistaken him for the trellis Romeo always climbed. . . .

He selected a Mozart cassette, switched his stereo on, then sat at his desk and studied a chess position he'd set up last night.

"Joshy!" his mother shouted from below. "I've been calling you for five minutes now! Are you playing chess?" She always seemed to know. Bad luck.

She was coming up the stairs. Joshua sighed and put the black knight down. If only he'd had four or five brothers or sisters for her to worry about instead of just him.

"No wonder you never listen," she said as Joshua unlocked his bedroom door. "The way you blast that stereo, Mozart is a public menace. . . . Joshy, I want you to get outside. It's an absolutely beautiful Saturday morning. Give the chess a rest for a change."

"Mom, please! Don't call me *Joshy!*" But of course she would. She would call him *Joshy* forever and ever, just as she had when he was three years old.

"All right, Mister Freeman! Is that better? . . . I'm

4

driving over to the shopping mall. Why don't you come on and join me—"

"But I have to be in New York by two for the tournament at the Metropolitan Chess Club—"

"Fine! You can get the New York bus from the mall, right?"

"Mom, please! I'm going over some games—"

"Just like your grandfather. Obsessive. I wish he'd never taught you the game in the first place."

"OK, Mom, I'll switch to three-card monte. I could make a killing on the sidewalks of New York."

"Very funny. . . . So you're not coming with me, is that it?"

"Not unless Folger's has that new chess computer in. You know, the one I asked you to look out for. The Grand Tour?"

"It's in."

"Why didn't you tell me?"

"Now I've told you."

"OK," said Joshua, taking his sweater from the closet. "I'll ride with you to the mall. But we're splitting up the minute we get there."

"Oh, thank God! You're ashamed to be seen with your mother! At least you're normal in *some*thing. . . . Oh, and listen: I'm going to be out till late, but there's cold chicken in the fridge if you get home before I do."

"Mom, I hate to tell you. I think the chicken is turning green."

"It is not!"

"Take a look."

5

"Never mind. Here, take ten dollars and get yourself a Chinese meal in the city. And if you're near Zabar's, Dad loves their smoked salmon. He wasn't in a very good mood this morning, and I think he might like—"

"But I'm not going near Zabar's. The chess club's on the East Side—"

"I thought you said you were going to visit Granma and Granpa this Saturday. Zabar's is directly on the way up to them from the Port Authority."

"Oh, *right*! I was going to play Granpa a quick game before the tournament. OK. How many pounds of lox do you want?"

"You don't buy it by the pound, Joshy. A half pound is enough. That stuff costs more than diamonds these days."

"Mom! Stop calling me *Joshy*! Please!"

"All right. All right. Don't get so excited. Though I really don't know what's so wrong with—"

"Mom!" Why was she so insistent? Why wouldn't she let him grow up?

"By the way, if I may ask," his mother said, "what's your underwear doing in the wastebasket, Joshua?"

"I guess there was no room in the pencil sharpener."

"Is that supposed to be funny?"

"Yes."

"Well, between comedy and chess, you'd better stick to chess. And stop throwing all your underwear out. The garbage men will think you're weird."

"They may as well," said Joshua. "Everybody else does."

2

Karen Hiler pressed a sticker onto the cover of *Hussy* magazine, obscuring part of the title and most of the nude woman kneeling in the cover photo. The yellow label read: THIS IS DEGRADING TO WOMEN!

"OK, that's five! Peel me another one, Lori."

Lori Lindstrom pulled the smooth paper backing from a sticker and passed it to Karen. "They're looking at us, I think," Lori whispered.

"Are they?" Karen turned toward the sales desk. "No, they're not. Anyway, who cares! Let them arrest us! . . . Keep feeding them to me, Lori!"

"Wait! It's hard to get the peeling thing started."

Karen and Lori worked their way through the stack of magazines in the topmost rack at the Condon Bookshop in the Lake Hills shopping mall. Karen had been planning this since Monday, when the packet of stickers had arrived at the local chapter of Women for Women.

"Hey, look," Lori whispered. "Over there. There's that boy Joshua, from history class. The one who's always reading a chess book. I drew a picture of him in class last week. He's got such beautiful black eyes. Just like yours."

"Who? Where?" Karen searched the bookstore.

"Over by the game books."

"Oh, him," said Karen. Why was she suddenly nervous, she wondered. OK, she'd noticed him in class, a little. He dressed like a nerd, and she liked that. And OK, he seemed sort of shy, and she liked that, too. Not like Mark had been. And he could be funny when he bothered to say something in class. And maybe he was, in a strange way, cute. But she wasn't about to get hurt again. Mark had been enough. *And* her father leaving, just like that. She needed a vacation from hurt. So forget *nervous* and switch to *who cares*.

"He's still looking this way," Lori said. "I think at you. He likes you, I bet."

"Lori, cut it out!"

"But he's nice. A lot nicer than Mark was."

"How do you know?"

"He is. I can tell," said Lori. "I wouldn't draw a picture of him if I didn't think he was nice, right?"

"You draw pictures of me. Am *I* nice?"

"Sure," said Lori, picking at the backing on the next sticker.

8

"I am not. Ask my mother. . . ."

Joshua watched them hesitantly, looking down at a chess book, then back at them. Karen Hiler and Lori what's-her-name. From history class. What were they doing with that magazine? Should he go over? Maybe start talking? He'd browsed through a copy once, himself. But why would *girls* be interested? He had heard someone in the locker room call them the homo twins. Could that be it? But even if it was, so what? He liked them. Karen who, again and again, pointed out places in the history text that she claimed gave a distorted view of women. Always arguing with Mr. Curtiss, the history teacher. Always wearing the same scruffy jeans and collection of buttons: NO MORE NUKES; PEACE POWER; WOMEN FOR WOMEN; on and on. Her dark-brown hair and large clear eyes were honest. That was the word: honest.

And Lori. Lori sat to his right in history. While Mr. Curtiss had talked endlessly about the Federalist Party, Joshua had seen her draw a long chain of entwined daffodils over her paper. And then chains made from the word *daffodil* swirling through the flower chain like necklaces: *daffodil daffodil daffodil daffodil daffodil daffodil daffodil.* He remembered the slight shock he'd felt as he'd peered at her desk and seen the words in the chain grow larger and larger, changing to *daffodel daffydell daffyhell daffyhell hell hell hell hell hell.*

She was somewhere else, this Lori, just as he was. She among daffodils and hells, he in the Tartakover Variation of the Queen's Gambit Declined. Her blond

9

silky hair was always tied back in a ponytail, leaving her thin pale face looking childishly vulnerable. He'd wished he could comfort her in class, somehow, and tell her she wasn't the only one who was somewhere else. Not the only one. He was there, too. He liked her. But he could never imagine himself touching her. Holding her. Not to mention kissing her.

Karen was the opposite. Karen was real. Her face, her gestures, her body, even her arguments were all real and touchable. But she looked so serious right now, at that magazine rack.

He wanted to go over and say something, but he hadn't even seen the chess computer in Folger's yet, and he had to get that bus for New York, and besides, they'd think he was trying to flirt with them, which he *wasn't*.

Why, he wondered, why did he always have to analyze things? OK! No more psychology.

Joshua walked over to them. "Hi," he murmured.

"Hi."

"Hi."

He pointed toward a sticker on a cover. "Hey, what are you doing?"

"We're trying to stop the exploitation of women," said Karen.

"Oh. . . ." Joshua wondered what he should say next. "I'm—I'm in your class. Joshua Freeman?"

"Oh, sure," said Karen. "You always read a chess book while Mr. Curtiss moron-izes. Right?" She wondered if that sounded stupid. Moron-izes. That was really stretching a word to sound oh-so-clever.

"Yeah. I guess—you know—I really like chess a lot," said Joshua, painfully aware of his clumsy answer.

"I like chess too," said Lori. "It's really neat. When you hurt somebody, instead of a real war, it's all just a game. I like that. That's the way wars should be fought. So no one gets hurt."

"Well . . . but people can get pretty hurt losing chess games," said Joshua. "They think if they lose a game, it means they're not intelligent and, uh . . . But actually, a lot of it is training and practice and memorizing openings and analyzing games that were played in tournaments. It's like learning physics or chemistry. Are you a real chess player, Lori? I mean, do you play seriously?"

"I've played three games in my life. That's not very serious, is it?"

"You can't even, you know, really learn the rules in just three games. . . . Hey, do you play chess?" Joshua asked Karen a bit too eagerly.

"A little," said Karen. "I used to play with my father, a long time ago. I'm no good at all."

"You could learn with one of those computers," said Joshua. "That's why I came to the mall. They've got a new chess computer at Folger's, and— Would you want to go down and see it? I'll show you how it works, OK? Let's see how easy it is to beat." He had said it all in a burst, to keep them from being able to say no.

11

"Do you want to go, Lori?" asked Karen.

"I don't know," Lori answered. "Do you?"

"I don't know. We've got all these stickers. . . ."

"Are you into the women's movement?" asked Joshua.

"I'm into a lot of things," said Karen. "Like the environment and the nuclear freeze and all that. But my mother joined this women's group and she never goes to their meetings or anything, so I've sort of taken her place."

"That's good," said Joshua. "Yeah, those magazines and stuff are pretty bad. Except . . ." Joshua hesitated. "I guess guys like to look at women without clothes on, sometimes . . . like even in painting and sculpture and—"

"I'm not against *that*! I'd be crazy to be against nudity when it's natural, or it's in beautiful art, and all that. I'm against this sort of crap where women are made to pose with their legs wide apart so men can leer at them. Just because some women who really, really need the money pose like that, then men think that all women are inferior like slaves or garbage. Do you see?"

"Yes."

"Do you agree?"

"Well . . . why don't you say *some* men think like that?"

"OK. *Some* men. Now do you agree?"

"OK, then I agree. . . ."

"You do? Terrific! . . . OK, let's go play with that chess computer. Lori, is that OK?" asked Karen.

Lori nodded. Funny, Lori thought, how their eyes

12

were both so similar, Joshua's and Karen's. Dark, like the feeling of velvet. Like chocolates in a box. She hadn't been able to get Joshua's eyes right in the drawing she'd done in class. Well, she could never get Karen's eyes right, either. . . .

3

Joshua noticed that the salesman in the electronic games department was wearing a fake red carnation in his lapel. All the salespeople in Folger's wore carnations; it was the identifying symbol of the store. The shopping bags bore pictures of gigantic red carnations on each side, with a script *F* at the center of each flower. Even the sales slips had a carnation in the upper left corner. Joshua thought the entire idea was revolting. It was one of the few things on which he and his father agreed.

"This is a level-four computer," the salesman said. "It's meant for adults. Expert level. We had the president of the local chess club try it out last week, and he lost."

"Can I try it?" asked Joshua.

"Well, as I said, maybe that other model would be more for you. But if you really want to try this one, I can set the button for the lowest difficulty category, and—"

"Let's set the highest," said Joshua.

"OK, if that's what you want. It's your checkmate, right?" said the salesman as he pressed the ON button.

The computer came to life, with a chessboard and all the pieces electronically displayed in starting position. Joshua keyed in his first move, and after a pause the machine answered with its own move, in dark-red display. Karen and Lori watched as Joshua explained that it was a standard series of opening moves called "book" because the moves had been analyzed in chess books. The computer took about twenty seconds for each move, but Joshua made his moves instantly.

"You can take your time, you know," the salesman said, as he walked over to another customer. "You're allowed time to think."

Joshua continued playing rapidly, making normal moves to test how "deep" the computer had been programmed to follow standard openings. On the twelfth move, the computer went out of "book"; it made a very ordinary move. Joshua hit back with a strong attack, feeling the power and confidence he always felt once he was behind a chessboard. He hoped Karen and Lori didn't think he was showing off, though he knew he was. And he also knew that all this time spent at the mall meant he wouldn't visit his grandfather that day. But he'd go next Saturday, for sure.

15

The salesman had returned. He watched Joshua play for a few more minutes, then again suggested that he slow up. "You're still moving too fast. This computer is very tricky. I've never beaten it myself."

"Check, you electronic retard, you," Joshua said, as he pressed some keys.

"Are you winning?" asked Karen, a little troubled. He'd sounded like her father just then, always having to prove himself.

"Sure. The computer is busted," said Joshua.

"Don't tell me you broke it," the salesman said. "You hit those keys too hard—"

"No. You know, busted? It means it lost."

"But . . ." The salesman hesitated. "Look. The computer has more pawns than you."

"That's because it took a pawn sacrifice. Now I can move in and force a checkmate. Let's see. . . ."

The salesman shook his head in disbelief and returned to his other customer. After a few more moves, the computer gave up. A message in dark red appeared on the display: CONGRATULATIONS! WE RESIGN! YOU'VE WON! NICE GOING! WANT TO PLAY ANOTHER?

"Not with an electronic retard like you," said Joshua.

Lori, who had been watching quietly, said almost inaudibly, "You—you shouldn't say that."

"Who me? What did I say?" asked Joshua.

"Retard. There's people who are really retarded, and they can't help it, and I . . . and I . . ." The edges of her eyes were reddening; she blinked rapidly again and again.

16

"I'm— Gee, I'm sorry," said Joshua, confused. "I mean I didn't . . . Do you have a relative who's— who's . . . ?"

"No," Lori said. "But people shouldn't say things like that. . . ." Tears were welling up now. She turned away, clumsily.

Joshua looked at Karen, searching for some answer or help. Lori was right; *retard* did sound ugly when you thought about it. But still, was it *that* serious?

"Come on, Lori," said Karen, putting her arm around her. "He didn't mean anything. Lori? Come on. . . ."

"Hey," said Joshua, toward Lori's back. "Look, I . . . I won't say that again. OK? I'm really sorry. Really."

"Lori, come on," said Karen. "You're OK. Maybe you ought to wash up in the women's room. It's at that end, over there. Should I come with you?" Lori shook her head no, and walked off in the direction Karen had pointed.

Alone with Karen, Joshua had to say something, anything. But what? All his confidence had collapsed.

"She's—you know—sensitive," he said.

"Yes. Yes, she is," said Karen. "She can be up, and then very, very down. Suddenly."

"Will she be OK?"

"Oh, sure. Don't worry. I've known her since first grade. She'll be fine." He *is* nice, thought Karen. He really seems to care.

"Say, I was wondering," said Joshua. "Do you . . . Would you like to learn how to really play chess?"

"Chess? Me?"

17

"I could teach you. I'm a pretty good teacher. Do—
do you want to?"

He seemed so eager and unsure and awkward. "Sure,
why not," she said.

"Well, I have to go into New York today," said Joshua,
"because I'm in a chess tournament and— Oh, brother,
I'm going to be late for my bus! But . . . would you be
able to come over to my house tomorrow? I don't have
to play in that tournament tomorrow; I have a bye. And
my parents are having some friends over from my father's furniture business, so they'll be out of our way.
And we can heat up a frozen pizza, and I'm very good
at milk shakes, and I've got to catch my bus or I'll forfeit
the chess match. Would you come over?" Had he said
it right? The words sounded so clumsy.

"OK. Sure."

"Great! My address is two forty-two Kenyon and—
how about—one o'clock? Do you sleep late Sundays?"

"Not that late. One is good."

"OK. Good. OK?"

"OK."

"I've gotta go! Tell Lori I'm sorry."

"I ought to say . . ." Karen hesitated, then continued. "I guess you can see. You have to be specially
gentle with Lori."

"I know," said Joshua. "I will. I really have to go.
So long."

"So long." Karen's face suddenly eased into a smile.

Was she laughing at him? Could she be just laughing

at him? He was making a fool of himself. And he was late for the chess tournament.

Or could she actually like him? It was impossible. She couldn't. She was being kind to him, as she was to Lori. Just kind. That was it.

"See you tomorrow," he called, and fled without waiting for an answer.

4

Karen wondered if she should tell her mother about Joshua. Maybe later. . . . She lit the tall red candle she'd bought at the shopping mall. When her mother came out of the kitchen, it would be a mini-surprise for her. She deserved a surprise. Her mother was great. Really great. Like Lori. Maybe that's why she liked Lori so much; Lori was a lot like her mother. Her mother never thought anything bad about anyone, not even *him*!

Him! Her ex-father. Leaving them for that twenty-five-year-old idiot, Diane, with her straight white teeth. Diane Lastman fitted in beautifully with her father's plans. The lawyer on the move, Mister Upward-Upward Hiler. Perfect for him. She matched his expensive Italian jackets and the new modern apartment in Manhattan. The apartment in which she, Karen, had almost thrown up the one time she'd been there.

Diane seemed just another part of his always having to win, having to be the richest lawyer in Lake Hills, the best tennis player, the best golfer, the best everything. Which hadn't left much time for being a father, best or not. When he'd been there for her, he'd been wonderful; true. How many times had he comforted her? But he was always gone again, out being first at something. Yes, he'd left them, in a way, before he'd really left. But he *had* left!

And her mother still talked to that man! She'd have him back, if he wanted to come back, which he didn't. Unspeakable!

Leaving her mother for that idiot! Her mother, who taught Shakespeare, Keats, even Chaucer to her seventh graders and explained it and made it all interesting for them. Her mother, who was such a great human being, even though she was obviously a supermasochist.

Karen stood back from the table as her mother came into the room carrying a salad bowl.

"Surprise!" Karen called. "Lunch by candlelight."

"Candlelight?" her mother said, as she placed the bowl filled with salad at the center of the table. "How lovely! Oh . . . but it's such a waste." She moved to snuff the candle.

"No, don't!" cried Karen. "It's rose scented. Can you smell the roses? I bought it at the mall. For you."

"For me? Karen, it's lovely. Yes, but well . . . we

21

could save it for an occasion when maybe we have guests over," she said in her slight accent.

"But this *is* an occasion. You and me!" Karen protested. "The only time you use candles at the table, the only time, is when there's men around. Like Mr. Fiorentino and Mr. Carson last week—"

"That was business, and you know it. Assistant Principals from the school aren't exactly men. Stop smirking! You know what I mean! They were my guests. You have to have a nice table when you have guests."

"Well, you sure don't do that for Rita and Barbara and Mrs. Rosten and all your other female friends, right? And the word *female* in female friends is redundant since you don't have any male friends because you're carrying some sort of a loony torch for *him*—"

"Karen, now you're starting something again!" Her mother took a step back, defensively. "I've made this nice lunch. You bought that candle, which is— I'm touched that you thought of me at the mall, but now you're starting—"

"Well, it's true!" Karen interrupted. "Mr. Carson obviously likes you—"

"Oh, don't be ridicu—"

"Yes he does! I could tell. Mr. Carson's divorced just like us— I mean like you— and he was trying to suggest going out to dinner with you and you acted as if you didn't hear him, and—"

"Karen! I have to live my own life my own way. You can't know what I happen to think of Mr. Carson."

22

"What's wrong with him?"

"Please!"

"Oh, crap!"

"You can do better than that kind of language!"

"It's in Shakespeare."

"It is not! I'm tired of your continually criticizing me because of Dad, and I—"

"Dad? What Dad? That word is no longer operative."

"He is your *father*, Karen. . . . If you're that concerned about me, then why don't you do something about your own life? Karen, I'm worried about you. The only close friend you have is Lori, who is so, *so* strange. She's obviously very bright and creative, and may become a marvelous artist someday, but she's so strange—"

"I've never heard you say anything like *that* before! Lori is great!"

"Yes, of course she is. But she's your only friend! Karen, you have so much to offer; you're so capable; you're so damned bright—"

"*Damned*, Mother? You can do better than *that* kind of language!"

"That *is* in Shakespeare."

"So is *Oh that a man can smile yet be a villain*, or something, which is my ex-father!"

Her mother shook her head and sat down, unable to argue any further. "I think you need some help. You're so angry at him—"

23

"Maybe *you* need help, in fact you *do*, because you're not angry at him at all. Why don't you go to a Women for Women meeting once and find out what's what!"

"Karen, I want to talk about *you*. Whatever was wrong with that friend of yours, Mark—and I agree, he wasn't such a nice boy, but still . . . Just because of him, and your father . . . Karen, are you never going to date another boy?"

Karen pulled a chair out and sat down. "Of course not," she said calmly. "Mark was over a year ago. Mom, why do you keep pushing me? I'm fine. . . ."

Karen's mother smoothed the tablecloth in front of her. She shook her head rapidly several times. "Oh, I . . . I'm concerned. I guess I feel Dad and I have messed up your whole life with this divorce, and—"

"Oh, Mom, come on! I'm actually going over to a living human boy's house tomorrow to learn how to play chess. How's that?"

Her mother looked up. "You are?"

"Oh, brother. Yes! You look as if you don't believe me. OK, I'll give you the vital statistics before you ask. His name's Joshua Freeman, and he's sort of a chess prodigy, and he can be very funny sometimes. He's in my history class. We met him at the mall today, me and Lori—"

"Lori and I," her mother corrected.

"Oh, Mom, for God's sake! And he's nice. Even Lori approves. See!"

"Couldn't you have said something about this in the first place?"

24

"You didn't ask. . . . Hey, Mom?"

"Yes?"

"Could we eat? I'm absolutely starved."

"So am I," her mother said.

"Oh, God, look at that! Mom!"

Karen's mother jumped. "What?"

"Did you mix mayonnaise in that salad dressing?"

"Oh. I forgot. . . ."

"I gained two pounds this week! My behind is actually not able to get into these jeans. And I—"

"Some feminist you are," said her mother. "You're not supposed to care how you look. Women's posteriors are meant to assume whatever size and shape the Lord intended."

"You're right! OK! Let's start lunch all over again. Take two! Hi, Mom! That tuna salad looks great!"

"It's chicken salad."

"Oh! That's different. I *love* mayonnaise in chicken salad!"

"Karen!"

25

5

Lori sat on the couch in the living room waiting for her mother and father and younger sister, Lisa. They were going to dinner at her aunt's home on Long Island that afternoon.

They were so slow. Well, she could sit quietly and think. About Karen and Joshua. And about tomorrow. Karen had asked her to go with her to Joshua's house. Was he going to become a friend? She hoped so. She liked him a lot. . . .

She shouldn't have cried at the mall, but she couldn't help it sometimes. Karen knew that, but Joshua didn't. . . . Karen and Lori. Karen, Joshua, and Lori. Karen, Lori, and Joshua . . .

Lori curled up on the couch to reduce her cramps.

Maybe she should just go to bed and disappear; the others were so busy they'd never notice. Lisa, eleven, was applying lipstick despite her mother's shrill objections. And her mother had been fussing with some eye shadow for half an hour. It was too dark, too violet, too cheap-looking. And her father had nicked himself shaving; something was wrong with the razor.

As always. Getting ready to visit. The same slow ritual, as always. Her family was so silly, pushing and jockeying for the bathroom mirror, and the sink, and the soap. Why not appear the way you really were? Why not say to the world: Hey, this is me. Bumps and all. Razor cuts and all. Scraggly hair, thin eyebrows, broken fingernails, and all. This is me. No, not me— this is my outer shell. My camouflage. Inside is the real me.

Inside is Lori Lindstrom. Look through my eyes, like through peepholes into a box. Take a look. There's a blue-green place, very quiet, very peaceful. And I'm there, hiding, small as a seed in a pomegranate, red like the seed, red. Because I'm menstruating. Because there's blood flowing out of me right now that came from a thought that didn't become a baby this month. Like in the Bible: and Sarah conceived and bore a child. Conceived . . .

Until Lori was ten, she'd thought that was how it happened, the way it was written in the Bible, or seemed to be: You sat down quietly and you thought and thought until you imagined a baby, and you conceived the child in your mind and the child became yours. It would be nice. It would be nice if you kissed a boy and he kissed you, and you sat together and conceived out of the air, like in sunlight, or in blue-green shadows, and then you would know, really know that he loved you, because together you conceived only because you wanted to, without wanting anything else at all.

She imagined Joshua and Karen together among trees, and herself there, too. All three of them, together, in blue-green shade, in tall grass, touching, all three . . .

Karen often said she envied Lori for her imagination. But it was more than imagination, Lori knew. It was real; more real than the room she was in. She could actually smell the grass, feel it under her bare feet, could hear Karen laughing, hear Joshua calling to them both, because he would love them both, and she, Lori, would love *them* both.

Her mother was staring at her. "Lori, please! It's time to go!"

"I'm ready. . . ."

"You look like you're in one of your dazes."

"I'm ready. . . ."

"Well, good," her mother said briskly. "We don't want to be late. . . . Oh, Lori! Couldn't you even brush your hair? Now I'll have to brush and comb it out for you in the back of the car. You are really so annoying sometimes!"

"I'm ready. . . ."

Joshua and Karen pulled her toward them; there were yellow flower sparks everywhere. And they conceived in the blue-green shadows, all three, as if it were a dance, a turning and weaving, a yielding and giving, while her mother yanked at her hair in the Ford station wagon speeding toward the George Washington Bridge and the Cross Bronx Expressway.

6

Joshua felt increasingly confident that he had a winning game. He stared at the chessboard, then back at Dr. Rudolph Klein. Klein looked worried; he had been studying his position on the board for over five minutes, even though he was in serious time trouble, with only eleven minutes left on his clock, for nineteen moves.

Klein's pieces were badly blocked. His slow, analytical game couldn't stand up against Joshua's constant pressure and unexpected forays. Klein was looking for the scholarly combination, the elegant resolution. Joshua played to win, never mind the style or flourishes.

But did he really have a "win"? He searched the faces of the half dozen men standing around the table watching the game, but they seemed impassive. Very good chess manners, but not revealing.

Winning game or not, Joshua knew he had to remain cool. No overconfidence. A chess game could easily be blown with a single bad move. Patience, patience, his grandfather always said. But the win would be so sweet. He would move up to third, behind John Valerian, the current U.S. Champion, and ahead of Tom Benziger, who had lost his game today. Tom Benziger, who at fifteen was the U.S. Junior Champion.

Maybe they'd report the game in *The New York Times*'s chess column. He'd never had a game in any of the chess journals yet, let alone the *Times*. Would that help convince his father and mother to let him leave school and concentrate on chess, as his grandfather had done long ago? It might. His father thought the *Times* was the last word in authority and prestige.

Tom Benziger was watching the game now, too. Hoping that Joshua would lose, no doubt. Well, he was winning!

Klein finally made a seemingly clever move that freed his bishop, but Joshua had foreseen it. He thought for a moment, then countered with a strong move of his rook into Klein's territory. Now there was a slight murmur from the crowd. It was going well. Joshua felt a surge of power flush through his thin body. The chess feeling, he called it.

Benziger said softly, as if to himself, "Questionable. . . ."

"Please!" said Joshua.

31

"We can't have comments during match play!" called the tournament director, Mr. Edelbaum. Edelbaum, the club secretary, ran everything meticulously and well, though he played chess meticulously and badly.

Could Benziger be right? Was it a questionable move? Joshua went over the alternate lines of development again, but he couldn't find any flaw. Maybe Benziger was trying to psych him out. Well, he had succeeded, because that confident chess feeling was gone.

Joshua had tried to be friends with Benziger once, as he'd been with Bob Kim. He'd tried. But Tom Benziger treated Joshua as if he didn't exist. He'd beaten Joshua several times in casual games at the club, then had avoided playing him again.

Benziger seemed to have everything. He was on his high school tennis team, and was half a foot taller than Joshua. And he had a girl friend who sometimes came with him to watch him play at the chess club. She was nice-looking. Very nice-looking. Painfully nice-looking.

Karen's face flickered in and out of Joshua's mind. Her face wasn't as pretty, no. But it was bright. Generous. Comfortable. It would be great if she'd go out with him. To have a girl friend. To be with her, to talk, to laugh together, to touch, to hold, to everything . . .

Klein had moved; there were groans among the onlookers. Something was wrong. Why had Klein done that? It was a blunder. Klein had once been an international master, had played all the greats, Euwe, Alekhine, Capablanca, but he was old, close to eighty, and was in terrible time trouble. Joshua felt sorry for him.

He reminded Joshua of his grandfather, so old now, too.

That move was the game. And any chance of getting into the *Times*. They wouldn't be interested in a game won by a blunder. It was painful.

If only Klein could see it and resign gracefully. But no; Joshua was being forced to take advantage of the blunder. He should enjoy going in for the kill, but he hated it. Klein was so old.

At moments like this, Joshua wondered what he was doing there. He didn't belong; he didn't have the real killer instinct needed for high-level tournament chess. He felt doubt spread through his body. . . .

Maybe his father was right; maybe chess was a high-class way of wasting time. Of wasting your life.

But he had to make the move. . . . Joshua looked at the people watching the game, then shrugged as if shedding responsibility. He moved his other rook, then hit the chess clock.

Klein nodded again and again. "So . . . finished!" he said crisply. He held his hand out to Joshua. He had resigned.

"Nice game," said Joshua shyly, but he knew it was emphatically *not* a nice game.

"Not so good," said Dr. Klein. "I'm getting old, my friend. Older every day and every night. We have to throw you young kids out of the club, what do you say, yes? Listen, tell your grandpapa for me, his grandson is a red-hot player. And ask him why he doesn't come down to the club anymore, hah?"

33

"OK, I will," said Joshua.

"And you remind him that I beat him in Carlsbad, 1929; Zurich, 1934; Moscow, 1935. All the big international tournaments. So now he sends you to get even, hah? Some trick!" Dr. Klein held out his hand again, and again, embarrassed, Joshua had to shake hands in victory.

Then Tom Benziger murmured, "Hey, that could have been defused. Knight takes pawn, bishop takes, then queen to bishop four, and the knight to rook six. See? Want me to show you, Dr. Klein? You could have equalized . . ."

Joshua felt a sinking emptiness. Damn! Benziger was right. Klein could have continued, but hadn't seen it. A double blunder for Klein, and an almost humiliating win for Joshua. Why didn't Benziger walk in front of a bus!

"Aha," said Klein. "Yes, I see. Very clever. Very, very clever. . . . Benziger! You should keep your mouth shut, because you make me feel sick. Maybe, though, I'll win the prize for the worst game in the tournament. What prize for that, Edelbaum? Hah?"

"A bottle of warm seltzer that's lost its fizz!" Edelbaum retorted. "And a write-up in *The New York Times*. Say, do you guys know that the *Times* is here today?"

"Oh, no! Where?" asked Dr. Klein.

"At Valerian's game, not yours. They're putting it in Tuesday's column. Valerian and Fleming, unlike you two, actually played chess today."

Joshua felt the remark burn like a hot needle under

his skin. . . . But still, at least he'd won. Third place, with only two more weekends left. Incredible! The glow spread through him; all the doubts were gone. After all, it was true: On the score sheet, a blunder gave just as good a win as a "brilliancy." . . . Third! Third as of now. Incredible!

And if he could beat Benziger next Saturday, and hold his own next Sunday, and by some miracle at least draw with Valerian in the final game, he could end up second.

If! If!

7

The doorbell sounded its two-note chime. Joshua raced to the entry hall to reach Karen before his mother could. He'd been anxious all morning about saying and doing the right things; about not looking like a total clod. But they were both there at the door, Karen *and* Lori. Both? But he had asked only Karen. He was certain he'd asked only Karen.

"Hi," he said.

"Hi."

"Hi."

It was clear to Joshua: Karen wasn't interested in him as a boyfriend. Not at all! She was neutralizing the whole thing. It would be three friends doing something together on a Sunday afternoon, nothing more.

36

"I—uh," Joshua stammered. "Come on in. I've— I've got some pizza ready to go, down in the rec room, and—"

"Great!" said Karen. "We brought some stuff, too. Lori made it; I just watched. Chocolate-covered apples. Don't laugh; they're really good."

They both had their small red backpacks that Joshua had seen loaded with books at school. The two of them, in their jeans and sweaters, were so fresh and full of good spirits that his spirits lifted, too. On other Sundays, he would have sat at the chessboard for hours, studying the latest tournament games reported in the chess journals. Sundays had been so empty since Bob Kim moved away. Girl friend or not, he was glad they were there.

Lori opened her backpack. "Oh, good," she said, as she looked through the contents. "The charcoal pencils didn't break this time. They're always breaking on me. . . ."

"I hope you don't mind," said Karen, "but I asked Lori if she'd come, too. She's not that interested in chess— right, Lori?—but she wants to practice sketching us. Is that OK? We were going to do something today, me and Lori—whoops! Lori and I! God, I hear my mother even when she's not around. . . . Anyway, I'd forgotten about that, so I asked Lor if she'd come here with me and . . . I should have phoned you first, I guess."

"That's OK!" said Joshua, relieved. Maybe Karen was interested in him after all. "I should have asked you both. . . ."

"I'll stay out of your way," said Lori. "I like to draw people, and you're people, right?" She giggled nervously. How could she tell them that when she drew a face or figure, the person became part of her own self, as if she'd received a transfusion of their blood from vein to vein.

"That's terrific," said Joshua. "I don't think anybody's ever drawn a picture of me. There's not much worth drawing, anyway."

"Yes there is," said Lori. "You're very 'drawable.' Some people are blah to draw, like Washington. I drew him for practice, and he was boring. 'Specially his mouth. But I think that Janis Joplin's face is really interesting. So's yours."

"Mine? Well . . ." Joshua hesitated, trying to find a way to mask his embarrassment. "That's probably because I massage my face every night with strawberry yogurt." Lori and Karen both laughed. Was it funny, or were they simply being polite? Always analyzing everything, again and again.

His mother had come into the entry hall. Disaster! He'd have to introduce everyone now. From the moment Joshua had told his mother that a friend would be coming over, a girl no less, his mother had been in one of her up moods, as if this would end the chess playing forever.

"Well, hello!" his mother called, almost singing it. "Oh, you have *two* guests, Joshy—Joshua! How nice to meet you."

Joshy! *Two* guests! Beautiful. How to turn your son into a nerd in one easy lesson.

"Uh, this is my mother. Mom, this is Karen Hiler and Lori—uh, Lori—"

"Lindstrom," Lori volunteered. "Hi."

"So nice to meet you both. Would you like some soda or some—"

"I've got stuff downstairs, Mom!"

"Oh, right! Yes," his mother said, retreating toward the living room. "Well, have fun, people. Maybe I'll see you later. *Ciao!*"

Even the *ciao* bothered him; his mother wasn't a *ciao*-type person. "Let's get downstairs to the rec room," said Joshua. "Fast!"

"You're sort of ashamed of your mother, aren't you?" said Karen, as they went down the carpeted stairs. "Maybe ashamed is the wrong word, but—"

"What! Who, me? No!" No one, not even Bob Kim, had ever said something like that. It was really blunt. . . . But it was strangely refreshing.

"That's all right," said Karen. "I'm ashamed of mine, sometimes. She's so masochistic. You wouldn't believe—"

"Well, I'm not ashamed of mine . . . I don't think," said Joshua, wondering if he actually was. His parents certainly were ashamed of him. The chess freak. The wimp. Well, he had a right to be ashamed in return. Share and share alike. He could probably find *that* in one of his psychology books, if he looked.

"But you made a face when she called you *Joshy*," said Karen, following Lori into the rec room.

"I can't stand the name *Joshy*, that's all. Hey," he said, trying to change the subject, "there's the pizza and shakes all set to go!" He pointed toward the built-in bar at one end of the rec room. There was a pizza next to a toaster oven on the counter, and a blender loaded with milk, syrup, and vanilla ice cream. "I've been ready for half an hour," said Joshua sheepishly.

Lori sat on one of the bar stools and started swiveling back and forth. "I wish you liked *Joshy*. It's so—I don't know—friendly."

"Hey," said Karen, "how about *Josh* instead?"

"Maybe . . ." said Joshua, sliding the pizza into the grill. "Nobody ever really called me *Josh* except one teacher back in fifth grade."

"You're kidding!" said Karen. "*Josh* is good! Josh Freeman. It sounds like *you*."

"It does!" Lori said, catching Karen's enthusiasm. "It really does, Josh."

"It does? I don't get it," said Joshua, as he pressed the start button on the blender. "What's this *me* that Josh Freeman sounds like?"

"Nice!" Karen said, over the blender's buzz. She hoped he could tell she meant it.

Joshua felt embarrassed again. "Thanks. . . ." He pulled the rack from the grill and sprinkled grated cheese over the pizza.

"Oh, that pizza smells so unbelievably good," said Karen.

"I added chunks of salami and some anchovies. I hope you like that sort of stuff," said Joshua.

"As long as you didn't add any strawberry yogurt," said Karen.

"Oh, no! I forgot! I used it all up on my face!"

"Well, how about adding chocolate apple crumbs, instead?" asked Lori, with her little nervous giggle that seemed an apology for speaking.

"Right on! That goes with everything!" said Karen. "Let's unpack them."

Joshua poured the milk shakes into tall paper cups, slid the pizza slices onto paper plates, then dealt everything out as if the food were playing cards. "One for you, and one for you, and one for me. And for you, and for you, and for me."

As they sampled the pizza, Karen cried out, "Ahh! It's hot!"

"Umm" was all Joshua could answer with his mouth full. Beyond some floor-to-ceiling windows, he saw the sun suddenly break through the cloud cover. The back lawn lit up from right to left as the clouds moved. "Mm-umm," said Joshua, swallowing the huge bite of pizza. "Hey, we could have this out on the picnic table. We could play chess there too, if you want."

"Oh, great!" said Lori. "A picnic! I love picnics!"

"Let's do it!" said Karen.

They gathered the cups and plates and carried everything outdoors. Joshua returned for the chessboard, carrying it like a serving tray, with the pieces all in place.

41

"Music!" Karen said. "We need music. Do you have a portable, Josh?"

"We have outdoor speakers. They're hooked to our stereo."

"You're kidding! Oh, turn on eighty-eight point one FM! They're mellow. They have good jazz."

"OK," said Joshua. He turned and walked back to the house.

Karen wondered if she was taking over. Her mother had warned her that she took over things sometimes.

"Lori, do you think I shouldn't have asked him? I'm always doing things like that. . . ."

"But music's great with a picnic," said Lori.

"Now his pizza's getting cold and his milk shake's getting warm. I'm dumb, Lori."

"You like him, don't you?"

"Uh-huh," Karen murmured.

"Me too."

"As a friend," Karen said quickly. "Just a friend." But was that true? she wondered. Or was there more going on? . . . He was bright; he was funny; he was gentle. He was what she'd said: nice. "Maybe more than a friend," she added.

"I know," said Lori sadly. How could she tell Karen she felt that way too. About Joshua. About her. About both. She couldn't. She couldn't. Karen wouldn't understand. No one would. . . . Lori stirred her milk shake with her straw. It would be all right. It would. She could be as close as she liked to Joshua, and Karen, too, within herself, where it was safe. It would be all right. . . .

Joshua hesitated outside the living room. He'd have to disturb his father and mother and their friends in order to reach the stereo equipment in its aluminum-and-glass cabinet. Worse, he'd have to say *hello* now to everybody in the room, and be introduced to those he didn't know, and make small talk. Maybe he could escape with a quick sweeping *Hi.*

"Uh, hi! Hello . . . I just want to turn on the radio for the outside speakers—"

"Say, Joshua!" his father called across the room. "How's your party going?"

"OK."

"I hear you have two girl friends over the house. Isn't one enough?" his father said for everyone to hear.

Joshua felt sick to his stomach. His father, usually very quiet, was showing off. Showing that the weirdo son was really an all-American lady killer, and not just a screwball freak. . . . His mother looked at him guiltily; she had obviously reported back.

Joshua tried to keep his thoughts cool and calm, as in a chess match. He set the radio for 88.1 FM and switched it to the outdoor speakers. OK. He would get out of the room fast, before there was another announcement from his father.

"Hey, Joshua," his father said. "You know I'm only kidding." His father had read his face. Well, it helped a little.

Joshua returned to the back lawn, to the sound of a jazz trio.

"Hi! The music's great," said Karen. "But I shouldn't have bothered you. I'm such a pain."

"No, it's a good idea," said Joshua. "I like music; it helps me concentrate when I study chess."

"Oh, that's right," said Karen. "When do we do the chess thing?"

"How about now?" said Joshua. "Soon as we finish the pizza and chocolate apples."

As Joshua started describing the moves and basic rules to Karen, Lori retreated to the far end of the picnic table to sketch. Joshua found himself entranced once more with the richness of the game and with the pieces that seemed to have personalities of their own: the stiff and stubborn rooks, the haughty queen, the tricky knights, the slightly eccentric bishops, and the hapless, but hopeful, pawns. He recalled his grandfather teaching *him* the moves in his crowded old-world apartment in uptown Manhattan, a glass of steaming tea at his side.

"See," said Joshua, "the pawn can become a queen. Like my grandfather said to me once, chess isn't only about war. It's—what did he say?—it's how the caterpillar can become a butterfly. How the least can become the greatest."

"He sounds like a very OK person," said Karen.

"He is. He's terrific."

"I wish I had grandparents living, but I don't."

Should he ask her if she'd like to meet his grandfather? And his grandmother? They could go there before the chess tournament next Saturday. They could

44

have a whole day in the city. Could she go? *Would* she go? But what if she asked Lori to join them again? Neutralizing it again. Well, he would try anyway. He'd ask her. Maybe at school. If he could just see her alone.

"Don't move! I'm drawing your shoulders!" Lori called to him.

Joshua laughed, and they, infected, laughed too.

"OK! You can move again if you want."

"Can we see your drawing yet, Lori?" asked Karen.

"OK." Lori turned the charcoal sketch toward them.

Yes, they were there, Joshua and Karen, leaning over the chessboard. Lori had drawn him holding a knight. It looked like them, thought Joshua. It *was* them. It was better than good; it was fantastic. But the chessboard wasn't a chessboard. It was, rather, a face. A face flat on the table. Lori's face, smiling. Weird . . .

"That's—that's interesting," said Joshua. "It's really good!"

"Surrealistic," Karen added.

"Do you like it, Josh?" asked Lori.

"It's terrific!"

"If you like it, you can have it," said Lori.

"Really?"

"Sure. Here." She handed him the sketch.

"Thanks. Thanks a lot."

"Hey, look! There's a bee sitting on that bishop!" Lori pointed to a black bishop on the board.

"They like the chess set," said Joshua. "It's because of our fingers. The pizza and chocolate-coated apples."

"You know," said Lori, "they should change the rules

45

and have little white and black caps. To fit the bishops, right? And if the other person is losing, you could turn your white bishop into a black bishop by putting a black cap on it. To help the other side."

Joshua shook his head. "But . . . then nobody would win."

"But nobody would lose either. Right?" said Lori.

"I don't know. There'd be no reason to play," said Joshua.

"Oh yes there would," Lori answered. "You'd play to be friends."

"Right on!" said Karen.

It seemed so naive and unreal. Yet a tiny hook of truth caught Joshua and wouldn't release. To play to be friends, and nothing else. That's how he played his grandfather, he knew. But *only* his grandfather.

"Maybe you're right," said Joshua, half wishing he believed it, yet knowing he didn't.

"Of course she's right," said Karen. "Lori is always right. Right? All together now. One—two—three. Rii—"

And all three yelled in chorus: "RIIIGHT!"

8

It poured Monday morning, a fierce rain that rattled on the school buses like spilled gravel. The buses moved blindly ahead, ten minutes late, picking up students thoroughly soaked from waiting in the downpour. All morning the high school corridors smelled of boots and damp rain jackets jammed into the lockers lining the walls.

As he walked down the musty hallway from his biology class, Joshua spotted Karen and Lori together, moving with the crowd. Their damp backpacks, slung over their shoulders, were heavy with books. He dodged and maneuvered past oncoming students to reach them.

"Karen! Lori! Hey, wait up!" he called.

As they stopped and turned toward Joshua, the stream

47

of students moved around them, barely avoiding collision. "It's Josh!" called Lori. "Hey, happy Monday! Nice weather!"

"Hi. My boots are waterlogged," said Joshua. "Where are you heading? I've got lunch next. How about you guys?"

"I'm stuck with math," said Lori, wrinkling her nose in disgust.

"I've just got a study period," said Karen. "I can cut it and go to lunch with you. No problem. I've done it before. I'm going to walk Lori to her math class first, OK? Come on."

"OK," said Joshua. Then more hesitantly, he added, "That—that was fun yesterday."

"I loved it," said Lori. "We were just talking. It was great. We're lucky it didn't rain then. If it's got to rain, let it be Monday, right?"

"We—we can do it again," Joshua continued, feeling his confidence slipping away.

"We could go and do it over my place," said Karen. "Maybe next Sunday."

"Sunday? Next Sunday? I can't," said Joshua. "I've got a tournament game on Saturday, and two more on Sunday."

It was hard to talk as they moved with the crowd through the hallway, but he would ask her the minute they were alone. For a date; a real date. He would at least try. But how, exactly? He'd thought about it for hours Sunday night, rehearsing dialogues, trying to find answers to every possible objection she could have.

48

Crazy. Crazy. Like chess, trying to cover every possible move.

They walked slowly toward the far end of the building. It felt strange. He'd walked along that hallway a hundred times since the start of the freshman year, but always alone, slipping around people on his way to his next class, making it something of a contest to see how quickly he could arrive. Now that there were three of them, the headway was slower. But he noticed, as if for the first time, other groups of twos and threes and fours walking slowly together. All that rushing past people—had it actually been to prove that he was better off alone? That he could move as cleverly as a chess knight around obstacles, alone? But it wasn't better. There was a smooth good feeling in walking with friends of his own.

Two boys he recognized from gym stared at them as they approached. What were they looking at? As they passed by, Joshua heard one of them call out, "Hey, there they go! The three weirdos!"

Karen and Lori had heard it, too; everyone in the corridor could hear. As the boys turned back toward them to examine the effect, Karen paused and turned, too, then held her fist out toward them and pointed her middle finger into the air in a clear message.

It was beautiful, Joshua thought. Girls didn't do that; shouldn't do that. But she had done it perfectly. She had such guts! And somehow it seemed to be aimed at protecting Lori. At being her advocate.

"Idiots!" said Karen.

49

A bell rang down the hall, but they had stopped paying attention long ago; half the time the bells didn't seem to make any sense. There was a myth in the school that the system of bells and buzzers was run by a teacher who had gone berserk from student harassment. Everyone called the imaginary bell keeper the Hunchback of Notre Dame.

"Thanks for walking us, Josh," Lori said just outside her math class.

"Oh, sure . . ." Joshua answered. "Don't let those guys bother you."

"Don't worry," said Lori. "It doesn't matter. I don't know about you, but I *am* a weirdo."

"You are not!" said Karen. "Doesn't anything ever get you sore? You're *you*! Don't let them win, Lori!"

Lori shrugged. "OK . . . See you later." She shrugged again, and joined the others going into the math room.

"Those—those clones!" said Karen, still angry. "Come on. Let's go eat, Josh."

The cafeteria was mobbed, but they managed to find two seats in one corner, near the tray-return window. Karen took her lunch out of her backpack and offered half of everything to Joshua.

"I always buy something," he said. "I think they have heros today."

"Gar-baage!" said Karen. "My stuff's healthier. My mother's salmon salad with yogurt. Best in the West."

"I don't know. I like hero sandwiches."

"Well, I guess you can handle calories. Your rear end looks OK. Mine doesn't."

He felt warmth creeping into his face, but he decided to say it anyway. "I don't know; yours looks pretty good to me."

Karen hesitated, trying to decide whether that was sexist or not. She put on a mock Southern-belle voice. "Oh, you ahh such a caution, Mista Freeman!"

"Huh?"

"With yo fancy words."

"All I said was— Never mind."

"No, say it."

He knew his face was turning red now. "All I said was . . . I think you shouldn't worry about calories, because—because you don't have more than you should have where you have it. How's that?"

"Surreptitious."

"You don't have too big a behind! Is that better?"

"God, yes! . . . You're blushing."

"So what! . . . I think I *will* have some of your salmon salad," Joshua said.

"Good. . . . How come you changed your mind?"

"I don't know. I don't want to waste time standing on line, I guess."

"Good reason," said Karen, handing Joshua half of her sandwich.

"And I'd rather be talking to you."

"Oh. Better reason."

"Karen? . . ."

"Yes?"

He hesitated for a moment. What if she said *no* to a date? He took a deep breath. Just go for it, he thought.

51

"I have to go into New York again next Saturday, and also Sunday, for this chess tournament I'm in, and—would you like to come in with me next Saturday and watch? The tournament? It's really interesting, and you could meet my grandfather before the match. Meet him and my grandmother, that is. And then we could go for pizzas or hamburgers, and have fun. All day. In New York. Would you?"

"Let me think." Could she go without Lori this time? Karen wondered. This was really a date, wasn't it? Of course it was. Well, she had the right to go out on a date, like anyone else. Lori had been OK most of the time when she had gone out with Mark. . . . Except Lori hadn't liked Mark. At all! This was different. Joshua was Lori's friend too. But not *boyfriend*. Lori didn't even want a boyfriend. Or did she? She was so confused, Lori. So mixed up all the time. . . . Well, maybe Lori did like Joshua, but Karen obviously liked him more, and that was that! She was going to go out with him. But maybe first in a smaller way. Not all day first. So Lori could see it wasn't such a big deal. And so Joshua didn't think he owned her. Good idea. Great!

"Hey," said Karen, "why don't we go out during the week once? Maybe—you know that old-time movie series at the mall on Wednesday nights? I was going to go and see *King Kong*. I saw it once on TV, but I want to check it out again. I'm planning to do an essay for English on antifeminism in it. Fay Wray always so helpless and all that baloney. You want to go? I'll make popcorn."

52

"Oh. Yeah—yes! Great! . . . With . . . with Lori, too?"

"Maybe not with Lori. . . ."

"OK . . . but how about Saturday in New York?"

"Can I tell you Wednesday night—or, say, Thursday?"

"Sure." Why couldn't she answer right now? But at least she was going out with him to a movie. That was a date, right? He'd done it! . . . But what did he say now? His dozens of practice dialogues hadn't gone beyond *yes*. If he played chess this way, he'd lose every time.

"This salmon salad tastes kind of sour," he said.

"It's the yogurt. It'll grow on you."

"Oh. It's good. Sour, but good. . . ."

"My mother made it."

She'd already said that, he noticed. Maybe she didn't really know what to say, either. They were going to go out together, but they were afraid to say anything about it. Well, he could be blunt, just like she could. He was going to say something.

"Karen, I . . . I'm glad I met you at the mall."

"Me too."

"I'm really glad. I mean it." He was looking right at her, watching her eyes now.

"So am I." She stared right back.

"Wow!" he said. The word felt loaded with enormous significance.

"Double wow," she said.

"Whatever wow means," he added.

"It means a lot."

"I know. . . . Boy, we're talking without even talking. . . ."

"I do that sometimes with Lori. . . ."

She smiled and then they both laughed, embarrassed at being embarrassed. It was strange. Why did he feel that every word, every slightest look, was suddenly so important, as if an electric needle were etching it into his mind forever?

"What are you smiling at?" he asked.

"Nothing. What are *you* smiling at?"

"The same nothing you're smiling at."

Karen slapped the table with both palms, as if she were making a firm decision. "OK, Josh! We're going to go out together. Boy meets girl. I like you. You like me. Right? Right. That's that. Period. The end. Now we can finish our lunch."

She *was* blunt. And maybe that was good!

A bell rang in the cafeteria. "Yikes!" said Karen. "The Hunchback of Notre Dame says it's time for history. Let's go."

"That's not for history," said Joshua. "It's only half past. That's for the hunchback's siesta time. The rain kept him awake this morning."

"Oh, you're right. . . ."

As the conversation faded, Joshua felt uncertain again. What could he say now? He couldn't think of anything funny. And if he became serious again, maybe she'd think he was a real jerk. He could ask about Lori. No.

54

Not now . . . . He felt paralyzed. Say something, idiot! This is supposed to be your girl friend.

"Hey! I've got my pocket chess set with me," he said. "You want to try a quick game? I'll give you some more pointers." Idiot! Idiot!

"Oh. Well, if you want to."

"It's a great game once you learn it. Actually, it's much more than a game. It's—it's like life." Idiot!

"Only life is like life. Right?"

"No, chess is, too. You'll see. Anyhow, we should play just for our audience. Which is the rest of the cafeteria. If people think we're weirdos, we might as well act like weirdos. We'll be the only people in the cafeteria playing chess during lunch."

"You're right!" said Karen. "Get out the set!"

"Hey, you like being weird, don't you?"

"Like it? I *love* it! Let's play."

9

Karen and Lori sat on the rug in Lori's bedroom, using the side of the bed as a backrest. They dipped into a bag of sunflower seeds set between them, with a bowl for the husks. Joni Mitchell's voice filled the room.

"She's really mellow," said Karen.

"Sometimes I cry when I listen to her," said Lori, tossing a shell into the bowl.

"God, you always cry. I'm sorry, but—well, you do. Can't you control it at all?"

"I guess it's like bed-wetting," said Lori with her giggle. "I can't help it."

Karen sat up abruptly. "You don't—Lori, you don't wet the bed, do you?"

"No! . . . But what if I did? Lots of kids wet the bed,

even at our age. There was even a story on TV. This boy always had to wash his sheets in the morning and hang them up to dry. . . ."

"Oh, I bet I know what *that* was," said Karen. "That must have been what they call a wet dream. It can get all over the sheets. Remember? We read about it in that dumb book my mother got me."

"It was not! It was plain ordinary bed-wetting. . . . But you know, it must be really weird being a boy. Did you ever wonder what it would be like to be a boy? And have wet dreams? Yich."

"It's not yich. It's supposed to be normal. Why don't you ask Joshua what *he* thinks about it?"

"Oh, sure, right away! . . . But . . . you know, Karen, sometimes I guess I really wish I was a boy. Don't you?"

"No! That's the trouble with women. They're not proud to be women. Say, that reminds me, I want to finish doing the stickers at the bookstore in the mall."

"But haven't you *ever* wanted to be a boy instead of a girl?" She seemed so insistent. It wasn't like Lori; she usually just let the conversation drift.

"I don't know. I guess I don't have your imagination." Karen scooped up some more sunflower seeds and twisted up her face to concentrate. "Maybe when I was younger . . . Oh, I remember! Once when I was maybe four or five we went to Denmark; you know, my mother was born in Denmark. I wish we could go again. Anyway, on the beaches there all the very little kids run around naked. And my two cousins, they're both boys, were there of course and I guess I envied

57

them, because they had more than me. I thought! I wanted to be a boy for about a day. Big deal, one day. Freud wrote all about that, but Freud was a male chauvinist. *He* made it into the biggest deal in the world."

"Oh, I don't mean *that*. . . . I mean . . . I don't know what I mean." Lori sighed and leaned back against the bed. "If I was a boy . . . I . . . I don't know."

"What?"

"Well . . . then I could go out with you. That would be neat." Lori sucked in her breath. Why had she said it? She hadn't meant to. It had just come out. Oh, Karen!

Karen stared straight ahead at the stereo. Lori had said things like that before in a vague way. But this time it wasn't vague. "But you *can* go out with me. We go out all the time."

Lori bit her lip. Go on. Go on. Oh, Karen! "Uh-huh. But—but you know what I mean."

"I *don't* know. . . ." Karen paused. But she did know. And Lori knew that she knew. "Yeah, I know, I know. I just . . . Lori, I'm not into that sort of thing. You know that. I just *can't*."

"I'm not asking you to!" Lori was sitting bolt upright. The record had turned off automatically.

"Oh. I thought maybe you were sort of hinting—"

"I am not! I—I just wanted to ask. . . . I wondered if you ever *felt* that way?"

"Maybe . . . once."

"About . . . about me?"

"No."

"Oh. . . ." Lori's disappointment seemed almost palpable.

"It was someone at summer camp," said Karen. "Three years ago. I followed her all over the place. She was a counselor. It was like a crush, that's all. . . . But I must admit, it hurt just as much as anything else. As much as Mark when he dumped me."

Lori shifted her position and studied Karen. "Then you *do* know what it's like?"

"I guess. Sure. . . . But that's the only time I ever felt that way. I was about eleven maybe."

"But what if you kept feeling that way? What if you followed a girl around in camp one time and a boy another time and—and it went on and on. Not just when you're eleven. When you're thirteen. Fourteen. Forever." So confusing. So confused. It was all coming out. Who cares; let it come out. Let Karen hate her. Let them all hate her. Her mother and father. Her sister. Joshua. Everyone.

Karen knew she had to be careful. Lori had never been so direct before; she seemed to be asking for help. She had to answer the right way. Exactly right.

"Well," said Karen, "if I was happy about it, I'd say great. That's *me*. But if I wasn't happy about it, if I felt I was an awful person—and it isn't awful at all!—but if I felt I was—if I was worried and bothered, I'd try to go to a psychologist. To help me not feel awful about myself."

"My parents won't let me go," said Lori softly.

"You're kidding!"

59

"They want to think everything is all wrapped up in little pink ribbons. . . . I don't know. Maybe I'm afraid to go. Maybe *I* want everything to be wrapped up in pink ribbons too."

"But did you actually ask them?"

"Yes. Once. When I was feeling really lousy."

"I didn't know *that*."

"I didn't tell you."

"Why not!"

"I don't know. . . ." Lori was almost in tears.

"Lori, please! We can't talk if you cry."

"You must think I'm awfully messed up, and I . . . well, I . . . I didn't want to . . . to turn you off still more."

"Oh, Lor, you *idiot*! I *love* you! You'll *never* turn me off!"

"Oh, Karen. . . ." She buried her head in Karen's shoulder and started sobbing. This time Karen held her and said nothing, letting her cry it out. After a minute or so, Lori took a snorting breath and reached out blindly for a tissue.

"Here," said Karen, handing her a bunch from the box nearby. "Blow your brains out. Dopey!"

"Thanks. . . . I'm . . . I'm sorry. . . ."

"Feel better?"

"Uh-huh."

"And they wouldn't let you go to a shrink?"

"They keep saying . . . that there's nothing wrong with me."

"You could talk to someone at the school."

"I could *not*!"

"Well, you could talk to me."

"I *am* talking to you."

"Oh. Well, I don't know if it matters, but I don't feel a bit different about you at all. I sort of knew anyway."

"But that's not really it!" said Lori. "It's not *that*. It is and it isn't. It's just— Sometimes I feel so unhappy. I just want—I just want to disappear. It's everything! The world is awful. It's like nuclear bombs. And all this disarmament stuff you talk about, and all that peace-movement stuff doesn't do any good. Because everybody's still killing everybody, and people hate each other. And my mother and father are so dumb. And my sister's going to be like them, I can tell. And everybody laughs at me. I want it to be nice, the world, but it isn't!" She repeated, softly, "It isn't. It isn't."

"I know," Karen said, soothingly. "I know."

"Do you?"

"Of course. Who doesn't? But I just roll with the punches more. You're too sensitive. You're like a— like an anemone. I saw some up in Maine. You know what they are? That sea animal that looks like a flower? You just touch it, just brush against it, and it closes up. Poof, like that."

"Am I like that?"

"Oh, wow, are you!"

"Well, at least I'm not like a . . . like a . . ." Lori searched for an example. "Like a pineapple tree."

"A what? What's that like?"

"I don't know. I just thought of a pineapple tree."

"Do you know why, Lori? Seriously! It's really Freudian—may I be forgiven for mentioning his name."

"No, why?" Lori's mouth turned slightly upward in anticipation. When Karen frowned like that, it meant a joke was coming.

"Because there happens to be a whole pineapple in your refrigerator. I saw it before."

"Oh, let's have some! I'm in the mood!" Lori giggled as if nothing were wrong. Could these sudden changes be the real problem? Karen wondered. These sudden crazy ups and downs?

In the kitchen, cutting open the pineapple, Karen wondered whether it was a bad time to talk about her going with Joshua to the movies. And New York, too. Lori seemed fine now, but . . . Maybe a little later. Still, she had to tell her. Somehow, she had to ease it to her.

"This pineapple's great. What will your folks say when they get back, though?" Karen asked. "We're destroying it."

"That's OK. My mother wants me to eat a lot. She thinks I'm too skinny. I don't fill out a bathing suit properly, is the way she says it. She means I'm flat chested."

"No, you're not. Anyway, I fill it out too much. Too bad we can't trade about ten pounds."

"I wish I looked like you in a bathing suit."

"Come on! I overflow," said Karen.

"I'll bet Joshua will like that, though."

62

"I'm going to have to lose weight. . . . You're laughing at me."

Lori tried to suppress her smile. "No, it's just that you jumped the minute I said Joshua."

"I did?"

"Uh-huh."

"And I shouldn't care what he thinks, right? Well, I can make mistakes. I forgive myself. Karen, you're forgiven. See? It's easy. You ought to do the same for yourself, Lor."

"I do." Lori cut another chunk of pineapple. "I'm so good at it, I can do it in my sleep."

Lori seemed normal now. Karen decided to tell her about Joshua and get it over with. "Say, Lori, speaking of Josh, I—well, he and I are going out on a sort of date on Wednesday. To a movie at the mall. Just a movie. Is . . . is it OK?"

Lori's face grew very still and waxen. "You . . . you don't have to ask me."

"I know, but Lori . . . I'm just trying to explain. We can all do something, say, Sunday—no, Josh has to play chess Sunday—maybe Friday, OK? We could all three do something Friday night."

"Josh is nice. I'm glad. I really like him." Lori's voice was flat and distant. The anemone was closing.

"Lor . . . did *you* want to go out with him?"

"Me? Well . . . I don't know. Me?"

"Because if you did—I mean, you could go out with him and I could survive. I mean, if he wanted to, and you wanted to, and—"

63

"Oh, no!" said Lori, breaking pieces of pineapple into shreds. "He's *your* boyfriend. He likes *you*."

"Don't be silly. He likes you, too. I can tell."

"Not that way. We're just friends. We're all friends. Right?" Her voice was flat. That's the way it was, she thought. That's the way it had to be. Only inside herself, she could touch them both. Hold them both.

"Of course we're friends. Oh, Lori, we are."

"Are you going to go to bed with him?"

Karen felt the question like a hand slapping her cheek. This wasn't like Lori. Was she jealous?

"Lori, come on. You know me better than that! First of all, I hardly even know him. Second of all, I'm only fourteen. Third of all, I don't believe in that unless you're really in love and old enough to know what the hell you're getting involved with, and all that bull. And fourth of all, what's biting you?"

"Nothing! So you'll just make out and fool around all over the place," said Lori.

"Oh, of course. Just like that. Until we get warts on our fingers or someone throws a bucket of cold water over us."

"I'm just asking! You don't have to be mean."

"Well, I went out with Mark and you never asked."

"It was none of my business. . . ."

"You're right! . . . Oh, Lori, come on! Mark and I really didn't do anything much at all. Not that he didn't try. In fact, that's why he broke off with me. And I *did* tell you! I remember now. . . . Lori, please. I don't know what's going to happen with Josh. I don't know. I just want to be able to go out with him. OK? Please?"

Lori nodded, tears at the edges of her eyes again. "Karen—I'm sorry . . . I didn't mean anything."

"I may as well tell it all at once," said Karen. "We may go into New York Saturday. To his chess tournament."

"It's OK. It is. Really, it is. I'm sorry. . . ." Her eyes seemed to be staring at something far away.

"We're going to have all kinds of fun," said Karen with enthusiasm. "The three of us, I mean. You'll see."

"I'm sorry. . . ." Lori had scarcely heard Karen's last words. She was running with them both somewhere else now, in a field she'd been to many times before, in the blue-green part of her mind. Running away from her room, her house, her town. Toward somewhere else.

"I'm sorry . . . I'm sorry . . ."

10

King Kong's enormous head filled the screen, threatening his captors with his gaping jaws. The giant ape was being forced into a huge cage; his roars reverberated through the theater.

"Yikes!" whispered Karen in mock fear, moving closer to Joshua.

"Hey, don't worry. I'll protect you from Big Boy," Joshua whispered. He put his arm around her shoulder, so lightly that it scarcely touched her.

"Oh, thank you; ah am ever so grateful to have you heah to pro-tect little old me," Karen whispered in her Southern-belle accent. "Oh, hold mah delicate hand!" She put her hand into Joshua's free hand and moved her head to his shoulder.

Joshua wasn't quite sure what to make of it. Was she being playful? Or was it just her way of getting closer? He hoped it was that.

"Are you comfortable?" he asked, trying to be casual.

"For sure. Your shoulder is exactly the right height. Are you OK?"

"Me? Yes!"

The side of her body seemed to blend with his, and her hair tickled his cheek. He was becoming erect. Could she tell? Her hand in his was almost at his lap. He tried concentrating on the movie, but it didn't help. He had to think about something else. Anything else. Something that was a real turnoff. How about his parents and their idiot comments when he'd told them he was going on a date? Why couldn't they be more like Karen's mother?

He'd met her mother earlier that evening. She was different, straightforward. Maybe that's why Karen was, too. *I'm glad you stopped by before the movie: I like to meet Karen's friends. Karen said some very nice things about you. And I hear you're an expert at chess. It's supposed to be a wonderful game, isn't it; the oldest game in the world, I think I've heard. We have a great chess master in Denmark; that's where I was born. Bent Larsen, have you heard of him? I'm sure you must have.*

No boy-girl stuff. No talking down. She spoke as if he were an adult, as if they were all adults. That's what was wrong with his father and mother. They treated him as if he were nine years old with some sort of first

67

puppy-love girl friend. His mother: *Oh, you're going on a date, Joshy—I mean Joshua. . . . Karen? Which girl was she, the dark-haired one or the blond one? . . .* King Kong? *What a movie for a first date! But it's kind of cute, in a way. It's so campy.* And his father, thinking he was being funny: *I'd have picked the blonde; oops, your mother is giving me a look. Well, I bet you'll learn to play some games beside chess with a girl friend, now.* Disgusting! Both of them! No wonder they couldn't understand his feelings about chess. They couldn't understand his feelings about anything!

Good . . . thinking about that had made him feel less aroused. But his hand was going numb in its fixed position on her shoulder. He relaxed, letting his hand slide down her side. He realized with a jolt that his fingers were against the side of her breast. In a sudden movement he pulled his arm away completely. He stared straight ahead at the screen, almost not breathing in embarrassment.

Karen shifted her position. She gently took his arm and eased it around her shoulder again. Was he afraid of her? she wondered. *That* was the sort of thing Mark had kept trying to do, and here was Joshua pulling away at the slightest touch. He was so—Not naive. Well, maybe naive. But more—just plain shy. And just plain nice.

Still watching the movie, she took his hand and guided it down to where it had been, to the edge of her breast, then snuggled against him in a silent language. She

68

would never have thought she'd do that, an hour ago, but with Joshua it seemed the rightest thing in the world.

Did she *want* him to touch her there? Joshua wondered. She pressed closer to him. He was surprised that he felt, not sexy or aroused, but rather, protective. She seemed so vulnerable. He pressed his head against hers in a sidewise nuzzling motion, while his hand touched her gently.

"I . . . Are you OK?" he asked softly.

"Mm-hmm. Are you?"

"Yes. . . . You're sure . . . it's OK?" he whispered.

"Yes. . . . I mean with you. Not anybody else."

"Oh. . . . I—I . . ." He searched for something to say, but he was too confused.

"We're missing the movie," said Karen.

"I don't care. . . ."

"Neither do I," she said.

From the row behind them, a woman's voice suddenly interjected. "Would you mind! I'm trying to watch the film. Why don't you two go in the back row!"

"Oh, God!" Karen whispered, as Joshua pulled his arm away again. "Good idea. Let's go back."

"OK," said Joshua.

"We're sorry," Karen whispered to the woman.

They resettled themselves in the last row. Karen guided his arm around her exactly as it had been, then put her head back on his shoulder. Joshua moved his hand slightly up and down as if he were petting a small child, gingerly.

69

"Mmm . . . Josh, what movie are we watching?"

"*King Kong* . . . I think."

"Oh, right. It's a great movie. . . ." She turned toward him, her face very close to his. "Super-great movie. . . ." Joshua kissed her quickly. They parted slightly, then kissed again, a longer kiss. Then parted and kissed yet longer.

Karen snuggled against his shoulder again. "Oh, wow . . . Whatever wow means," she said, echoing their words in the cafeteria on Monday.

"It means a lot," he said, repeating her words too. "Right?"

"Mm-hmm. . . ."

As he held her closer, her hand accidentally brushed his lap. She hesitated a split second, then moved her hand away. Was that an erection? she wondered. Good. It meant he was feeling sexy about her. Well, that's how she was feeling about him, too.

"You can . . . you can, you know, touch me there if you want," Joshua stammered.

"No. I don't think so. No. No way." She suddenly sat up straight. "Hey, we better talk," she whispered. "I mean, this is crazy. We've only been together like an hour or so, and whammo! Look at us! I'm beginning to see what they're talking about in this book my mother gave me. About having to control things."

"Sssh!" came from somewhere in the theater.

"Omigod, I hope people can't hear what we're saying," Karen whispered. "Let's get a pizza and talk. OK?"

"OK," Joshua whispered back.

At the pizzeria in the mall, in the glare of bright lights and shiny tables, they both felt awkward with their new closeness.

"How's your pizza?" asked Joshua.

"So-so. Mall stuff. Not like the one you made," said Karen.

"I guess mine was hotter, at least."

"So what do you think?" she asked.

"About what?" asked Joshua, not quite certain whether she was still talking about the pizza.

"Us. . . . We've got to watch it, right? I mean, we should talk about it. I believe in talking."

"I . . . so do I."

"I've never really done this stuff before," said Karen. "I'm worried."

"Why?"

"Because I think it's going to be hard to stop. And I like it. A lot."

"I know," said Joshua. "So do I. . . ."

"The female is supposed to set limits. Chapter three of the crazy book my mother gave me. Only I don't believe in that. I think the male and female should set limits together. . . . You know, you're right about the pizza. It isn't hot at all. It's beginning to taste like papier-mâché. In fact, I think it *is* papier-mâché. . . . So what do you think about limits?"

"Well—maybe we could do what we did tonight, but not much more. . . . How's that?" Why was he so nervous, when she seemed so matter-of-fact about it?

71

"I agree. For a while, at least. I can't really handle any more. I'm not ready for it."

"I—I guess I'm not ready for it either," said Joshua.

"Hey, I don't mean the real *it*. That's something else. I just meant doing even a little more, now. I'm not ready. I'm not."

"I know. Don't worry about it. I'm not either."

"So we agree?"

"Sure."

"Shake."

"OK."

They shook hands across the table, then burst out laughing. "We are nuts!" said Karen.

"Like those guys in the hall said: There go the weirdos. You, me, and Lori. The three weirdos."

"By the way," said Karen, "I can go into New York with you. But you know, I wish we could both do something with Lori soon . . . I really do."

"We could go to the Freshman Dance Friday night. How would that be?" asked Joshua.

"I hate dances," said Karen. "But we could go just to be crazy. It could be fun. With you there, too, I mean."

"Believe it or not, I've only been to one dance in my whole life," said Joshua. "In fact, I can't dance."

"That's OK. Neither can I. We'll make it up as we go."

"OK. We'll have a triple date, sort of. You, me, and Lori."

"Great!" said Karen. "Oh, there's something else. I

never stop. On our way home tonight, we bike right by Grier's Pond. You know, that little lake with the old beat-up bandstand? Could we stop there a minute?"

"Sure, OK. But why there?"

"Because ever since I was nine years old, I swore that the first real boyfriend I had, I'd want to kiss him there the first time we ever went out. It's my favorite place in New Jersey. Isn't that romantic?"

"I think . . . I think it's beautiful," said Joshua.

"And if that first boy ever turned out to be the *only* one, and we stayed together all our lives . . . when I was old, I'd want to go there again with him—Josh, what's wrong? You're—are you crying?"

"No! It's the pizza! I just have to sneeze!"

"Oh, my God! You're as bad as Lori! That's great!"

11

The blue banner over the main entrance to Lake Hills High School read: FROSH BASH! Joshua could hear the beat of electric guitars as he searched for Lori and Karen among the groups of students in front of the school. He thought he detected the faint sweet smell of marijuana in the crowd. He'd tried marijuana once in Bob Kim's apartment in New York; the burning in his throat and lungs had made him sick for days. Even now, the odor made him feel slightly nauseated.

As he strolled across the lawn at the side of the building, he saw Lori standing near the tennis courts, alone amid the throng of students. She seemed so lost, so out of place all dressed up in her white lace blouse and long white prairie skirt. Her clothing, her straight blond hair, her thin delicate face made him think of old photographs, in sepia, of frontier women in their Sunday best.

"Hi, Lori," he called.

"Oh, Josh! Where's Karen?"

"I don't know," said Joshua. "She said she'd meet us here. . . . Hey, you look really nice!"

"Oh . . . so do you," she said.

"Me? No, I just dressed like my usual nothing. Well, I've got a new sweater. . . . But that's really nice, what you're wearing."

"I made the skirt myself. . . ." She giggled her little giggle and moved her hair back from the edge of her face with her hand. The movement seemed to Joshua to be almost musical.

"That's terrific!" he said. "You draw. You make your own clothes. It looks like you're good at everything."

"Well, I'm no good at chess!" She brushed her hair back again. Why hadn't he noticed that gesture before? She'd always fixed her hair with a band in back, he realized. It looked better like this, flowing over her shoulders. Much better.

"I—I like your hair like that. Is it like a style? Or maybe—that's just the way it is, I guess."

She laughed. He'd never seen her this happy. Even her eyes were laughing. What was happening? She was so different alone with him. Was she flirting with him just a tiny bit?

"Karen's late," he said nervously.

75

"It's OK. She's usually late. Some people usually are. She goes crazy trying to get to places on time. . . . Oh, listen! You can hear the music from here."

"It's going to be very interesting," said Joshua. "I can't dance."

"Neither can I," said Lori. "Not this kind of dancing. But I took ballet for a while."

"You look like you'd be good at ballet," Joshua said. "You really look like a ballet dancer."

"That's what my mother keeps saying. That's because I'm skinny. Ballet dancers are supposed to be thin as rails. But I'm not as skinny as I look."

"Oh, I know. I didn't mean that—"

"Are you as skinny as *you* look?" Lori smiled and again brushed her hair back.

"I guess so."

"That's how a chess player's supposed to look, right? And I guess a cook's supposed to look fat. And a truck driver's got to be tough. And a poet's supposed to be a sissy. And everybody's supposed to be what people think they're supposed to be. But the thing is that people are what they are. And the thing is . . . the thing is . . . that I don't know what I'm talking about anymore." She laughed and did a clumsy dance step to the distant rock beat.

"We could dance out here," she said. "Oh, there's Karen!" She waved her hand. "Karen! Karen, over here!" she called, jumping up and down eagerly.

Even her way of waving and jumping seemed strangely out of place. As if she were terribly naive, a farm girl

76

who had never been to the city. But he liked it; it was so awkward and innocent. It reminded him of how awkward he often felt.

"Hi, guys! Sorry I'm late," said Karen. "Wow, look at you, Lor!"

"It's that skirt I made."

"It's great! And your hair. You look terrific! Doesn't she, Josh?"

"She does! You do, Lori."

"Oh, man," said Karen, "you can hear that crappy band right through the brick walls. They must have those speakers up to a billion decibels. . . . Oh well, gang. Shall we plunge?"

The blast of music threw a solid wall of sound at them as they entered the gymnasium. They joined the crowd standing around the edge of the dance area.

Joshua shouted into Karen's ear over the speakers' fire-alarm crescendo, "Hey, this is the pits!"

Karen screamed back, "It's lovely! You just don't appreciate good music!"

It all seemed fake to Joshua: the numbing music, the disjointed dancing, the garishly decorated gym. Yet at that moment among the pressing couples, it felt good to be there with his own girl friend, to be not the crazy chess player in the cafeteria, but one of the crowd, normal, average, unnoticed. To be a couple; to be twinned, paired. He put his arm around Karen's waist and drew her toward him. She automatically put her arm around his waist too, then, realizing Lori had been excluded, tried to pull free.

77

"Why don't you two go dance!" Lori called out abruptly, walking away.

"Where are you going?" asked Karen. "Are you OK?"

"I'll be back," Lori shouted over the music. She maneuvered between couples as she crossed the dance floor, then, seeing an open space, started dancing by herself. Joshua felt a rush of embarrassment for her; she was moving clumsily.

"Maybe I ought to go dance with her," Joshua shouted to Karen.

"Hey, wait! Look at that!" Karen called back.

A tall, muscular boy had walked over from the edge of the dance floor and begun improvising skillful steps to match Lori's. Within a moment he was teaching her, showing her a step, then repeating it with her.

Karen shouted to Joshua, "Hey, how about that!"

"I know that guy," said Joshua. "Eric Glastonbury."

"What's he like? Isn't he a senior?"

"I think so. I see him trying to make out near the sports equipment cage with a different girl every other week."

"Oh, great!" Karen shouted.

"Should we go over?"

"She's having fun. Let her be!" said Karen, as she watched them dance.

With a series of dissonant chords, the band swung into a hard-rock beat while the lights dimmed. A strobe suddenly began flickering. Everyone seemed to move in jerking slow motion in the stuttering, metallic light.

78

Couples disappeared and reappeared in new positions, almost at random.

Joshua and Karen tried to improvise some steps. The strobe light made the simplest movements seem different and exciting.

"Hey! We're great!" Karen shouted.

As the music's tempo increased, the strobe light's flicker also accelerated. Karen stopped dancing.

"I can't keep up with *that*," she called to Joshua. She looked around the gym, trying to see in the spasmodic light. "Josh, do you know where Lori is?"

"I think over there." Joshua pointed toward a far exit.

"Have they gone outside?" Karen pulled away from Joshua and quickly scanned the far end of the gym. "Josh, this strobe is driving me nutso! Let's go outside too!"

"OK!" he called as he followed Karen toward the exit, dodging and weaving past the dancers.

"Come on, Josh!" Karen started striding across the front lawn, searching among the crowd of students.

"She'll be OK," said Joshua, trying to calm her.

"I'm not worried about her!" said Karen defensively. "I'm just . . . worried."

They walked around the building, then over to the football field and back. At the far end of the tennis courts, several couples huddled in the shadows.

"Let's have a look," said Karen.

As they drew near, one of the couples turned and glared at them.

79

"Oh, sorry," said Karen. "Just looking for some-one. . . . Sorry. As you were. . . ."

"Hey, look! It's Mr. and Mrs. Lunchtime Chess!" called the girl. "And when are you two going to have some little chess sets?"

Joshua felt his body grow heavy with anger.

"Oh, I don't know," said Karen very calmly. "Maybe after *you* two have some little laughing hyenas. Mean-time, why don't you bag your face!"

Perfect. Nasty to a turn. He couldn't have done better in a million years.

12

The car was parked at the far end of the school parking lot, away from the overhead lights. Everything felt so smooth. The forties dance music from the car radio reminded Lori of silver gift wrap. She let her head rest back against the front right seat while Eric Glastonbury poured something from a thermos into her plastic cup.

Why had it hurt so much to see Joshua put his arm around Karen . . . and Karen's arm around him? . . . . So much. . . . Well, now they could be alone. Now she wasn't a third wheel anymore. . . .

To be Karen. If she could only be Karen . . . or Joshua. . . . To hold . . . to be held . . . She felt an ache as if sweet chocolate were just out of reach, behind glass. Not for her. . . . She sipped the bitter drink in the plastic cup.

"Hey," said Eric, "how do you like this stuff? Better than beer, right? Scotch and club soda. And heavy on the scotch. My dad's favorite. Only way to go."

If only he wouldn't talk. Who *was* he? Eric something. Eric Glasstone? Glasshouse? Glass Eye?

"Mmm," Lori murmured, sipping her drink.

"You're slowing up," said Eric. "Can't take more than two, huh?"

"Oh, I can," said Lori. "But I want it to be . . . smooth and slow and . . . and nice. . . ." She heard her own voice slurring the words. Was she getting drunk? Good. Let it come over her like a blanket. . . .

"Hey, OK!" said Eric. "Really smooth and romantic, right?"

"Mm-hmm. . . ."

Let him be Joshua. Josh. Joshy. . . . If she closed her eyes, he could become Joshua. And she could be Karen. It would be nice. . . .

Eric was kissing her. Nice. The bitter drink, and the kiss, so nice. . . . Joshua on Karen's lips . . . his arm around her . . . the music in the dark car like a bubble of silver air under the sea. . . . Kissed her again. Joshua's lips. Karen's lips. Floating in a bubble of music. Karen's lips. Smooth. Soft. Picture her eyes. His eyes. Like the dark centers of flowers. Eyelashes. Petals . . . She would draw them, tomorrow. She would draw the kiss . . . Karen's kiss. Joshua's kiss . . . Confusing . . . so confusing . . .

Eric's hand was at her crotch, suddenly, pressing through clothing, moving, rubbing.

Lori sat up abruptly, spilling her drink over her skirt. The cold wet cloth clung to her legs.

"Hey, what's the matter?" Eric asked.

"I'm sorry. . . . I—I thought you were somebody else."

"What! Who?"

"No one. I better go. . . ."

"Hey, come on! I was only trying to make you feel good. Come on."

"I better. . . I have to meet . . . to meet somebody."

She reached for the door handle, but the car door was locked. It was hard to focus. The latch release, where was it? She struggled with the handle again.

"I didn't mean anything," said Eric. "Hey, what's wrong with you?"

"I have to . . . I have to go."

"You looked like you wanted me to do that! Come on!"

"I'm sorry . . . I'm sorry . . ."

"The guys are right. You *are* a queer."

"Oh. . . ." Even through her numbness, Lori felt the pain. But no. Let everything become a blur. A blanket. A warm blanket.

As she stood, she had to hold on to the side of the car. The parking lot was turning like a giant carousel, cars for horses. . . . How long had she been there drinking?

The ground felt rubbery, soft. She walked from car to car, using the fenders and doors as crutches. There were too many cars. Was she going in a circle? The music. The rock band. Go toward the music.

"Lori!"

Karen was calling her. Where? Behind her. Karen. Joshua. Safe. They were safe. Like her old dolls. The silent friends . . . Voices. Hands . . . I love you both. I do. Oh, I do. . . .

"Lori, my God! Where were you?"

"I—I was just—having fun. . . ."

"Your dress is absolutely soaked!"

"Oh . . . it's wet, a little . . . I spilled . . . my drink in Eric's car."

"Oh, good grief!" said Karen, putting her arm around Lori's shoulder.

Please, thought Lori. Hold me like that.

Joshua moved from side to side, not quite knowing what he could do. "Karen, I—I think we'd better get her home. Can she walk?"

Safe voices. Safe.

"OK, Lori. Listen," said Karen. "You're going to walk between us. Josh, can you get her other arm? Like that. That's it. Come on. Let's get off school property, quick."

They walked along a side path, away from the crowd of students at the main entrance.

"Easy. Easy," said Joshua, as they went down some steps. It was strange; he'd hardly known Lori a week ago. Now, holding her, helping her, she felt like more than a friend.

"If I see that Eric, so help me I'll punch him out," said Karen angrily.

"No . . . no . . . please," said Lori. "It was—it was my fault."

"Oh, naturally!" said Karen. "It's always the woman's fault, no matter what happens."

"Oh . . . I feel sick. . . ."

"Lori, can you throw up?" asked Joshua. "Because if you could, that might be good."

"No . . . I don't think so. . . ."

"OK. Keep walking. Keep walking," said Karen. "We'd better go over to my place first. My mother's out."

"O . . . *K* . . ." said Lori, as if the answer were profound.

At Karen's house, Lori washed her face and neck with cold water at the bathroom sink, again and again.

"Ohh . . ." she moaned. "I'm stupid!"

"Feeling better, stupid?" asked Karen.

"Yes . . . I'm so stupid!"

"You sure are! Why would you do such a dumb thing? Getting bombed in a guy's car, a guy that you hardly know!"

"I don't know. I felt like . . . I wanted to—to disappear for a while. That's all. . . . Oh, I'm getting a headache."

"Great," said Karen. "Do you want some aspirin?"

"No. I just want to go home." Go home, now, she thought, and let them be alone. No more third wheel.

"Hey, we'll walk you, OK?" said Joshua.

"But I'm fine," said Lori. "I *am*. . . . I have a head-ache, that's all."

"You look pretty zonked out to me," said Karen. "Josh, I don't think I ought to be going into the city with you tomorrow. I think I'd better stick around and—"

"No! I'm fine!" said Lori. "If you don't go into New York with Josh tomorrow, I'll—I'll . . . I don't know what! I'm OK now. You want me to prove it? I'll walk a straight line down the block."

"This I've got to see," said Karen. "If you can walk straight down the block with your eyes closed, I'll go into the city. OK?"

"OK!"

"Deal?"

"Deal!" said Lori.

"OK. Let's go," said Karen.

On their way to Lori's house, they took turns trying to walk with their eyes shut. Karen and Joshua both stumbled, but Lori managed to go an entire block with-out staggering.

"See!" she called out. "You go to New York, Karen!"

"OK, but I'm stopping by your house in the morning. What time are we leaving, Josh?"

"Nine."

"I'll be by at eight."

"No! Everybody's still asleep at eight."

"Oh. Well, I'll phone you just before we leave. Quarter to nine. How's that?"

"All right, I guess. . . . Are my eyes bloodshot?"

"No. . . . But I've got an idea," said Karen, taking a roll of mints from her pocket. "Here. Better chew some of these before you go inside."

"Oh," said Lori. "Thanks. I think I'm going to have to barf after all! I better go!"

As Lori rushed into her house, Karen took a mint and offered one to Joshua. "Have a mint while we wait," she said. "I want to make sure Lori's all right."

After a few minutes, a light went on in Lori's bedroom. Karen sighed and nudged Joshua. "OK, we can go," she said.

As they walked slowly back toward Karen's house, she seemed lost in thought. She ate one mint after another, offering them to Joshua every so often. "I become a candy junkie when I'm worried," she said.

"All I do is bite my lip," said Joshua. "But it drives my mother crazy."

"Mm-hmm." Karen drifted back into her own thoughts again. As they continued walking, Joshua put his arm around her shoulder and matched his steps to hers. "Is there anything I can do to help?" he finally asked.

"I don't know," said Karen. "She's never done anything like this before. Getting drunk. What do you think? Maybe we should have done something else tonight. Maybe that dance wasn't such a great idea. . . ."

"I guess not," said Joshua. "But she seemed fine when I saw her before you got there. She looked really happy."

"She's moody. You've seen it, right? She can flip in

a minute. . . . Why would she do such a dumb thing? Getting swashed in a guy's parked car."

"Maybe she trusts people too much," said Joshua.

"Oh, brother, does she ever!"

They passed Grier's Pond, a remaining section of wildlife tucked in among the blocks of houses. Karen pointed toward a bench facing the pond. "My favorite bench again. Can we sit awhile? I'd like to talk. OK?"

"Sure."

A slat was missing from the back of the bench, and one of the concrete supports had been uprooted.

"This bench gets worse every single day!" said Karen. "Josh, I really wish Lori had a friend. I mean a boyfriend. God, I hate that word! A *male* friend. Joshua, do you—well, do you think you know anybody?"

Bob Kim would have been perfect. Why couldn't this have happened a year ago? Where had he read that everything in life was just a matter of timing?

"I knew someone last year," he said, "but I guess I don't now. I wish I did; I really do."

"It probably doesn't matter. I have a feeling Lori's not interested, anyway. I don't know. She's all mixed up. I wish I could talk about it, but I can't. She's just mixed up."

"Maybe she needs a psychologist. Or something like that."

Karen shrugged her shoulders. "Believe it or not, she wanted to go to one, and her parents wouldn't let her. Nice, huh?"

"I guess people still believe if you go to a shrink, it means you're nuts, or close to it. Like it's a big disgrace."

"It's all dumb," said Karen. "Everything's dumb. Lori's right; the world stinks. I'll bet we never get to be twenty-five; the bomb will take care of us all. So why worry about anything? . . . Neurotic, huh? I could use a shrink, too."

"That's not neurotic. I think the same thing, sometimes," said Joshua. "You know, if it wasn't for chess, I'd probably want to be a psychologist myself. I've read a lot of books."

"Really? That's great!"

"I wish I was one right now. I could help Lori. Even though you're not supposed to analyze friends. . . . But I've decided. Chess is going to be my main thing."

"Why can't you play chess and be a psychologist, too?"

"I'm not into chess just for a hobby. I want to get on the chess circuit and play in all the tournaments I can. It's like being a tennis pro. You can make a living at it. I've been trying to convince my parents—"

"It sounds . . . well, it's none of my business," said Karen.

"It sounds crazy, right?"

"I guess. But whoever said you were sane, right?"

"Right."

As it grew colder and darker, they huddled together on the bench, feeling each other's breath warm on their faces as they kissed. There was mint from the candy on their lips, on their tongues, touching. Tonight, for the first time. Touching. Secret, close. But . . .

What was wrong with him? He was holding Karen, kissing Karen, yet he'd had a sudden image of Lori, all dressed up in her white blouse and prairie skirt. Of Lori brushing back her hair with her hand. Lori drunk and helpless. Wordless images. Quick as shooting stars, then gone. . . .

He kissed Karen again, then stared at her, stared till she smiled, then laughed. Her good warm laugh. Her Karen laugh.

Yes, Karen. He kissed her again, mindlessly, urgently, tongues touching once more. Yes, Karen. Karen. Of course. Karen.

13

Joshua and his grandfather studied the chessboard, as they had so many times before, at the little table by the window of the apartment in Washington Heights. Karen squatted on the floor beside them, watching. The late-morning sun through the window made everything glow with pinpoints of light. His grandfather's shaky hands seemed to be toying with the light, feeling its texture between constantly moving thumb and forefinger. Parkinson's disease, his mother had said.

His grandfather's thin frame seemed lost in the large old chair with the broken post. Every movement was difficult for him, yet he insisted on handling his own chess pieces. Sometimes a piece fell and Joshua quickly righted it.

91

Joshua's grandmother was also frail. She moved slowly but firmly about the apartment, bringing everyone hot tea and sponge cake from the kitchen. She was always moving, arranging and rearranging the little bouquet of flowers Karen had picked from her backyard, straightening a lace coverlet, adjusting the window blinds, fixing and smoothing with boundless nervous energy. She pulled a chair over to Karen, letting it scrape along the floor.

"Please, Karen, you are the guest," she said. "A chair is much more comfortable."

"Oh, thank you; I'm fine. I really am," said Karen. "I sit on the floor all the time. I don't even have a chair in my room at home."

"But then how do you do your homework?"

"On the floor. Really!"

"Even when I was a child in Europe, I had a chair. Not such nice clothes, but a chair, yes."

Joshua looked up from his game. "She's OK, Granma."

"How do you know!" said his grandmother. "Chess, chess, chess, chess, chess. You have a pretty girl here, and all you look at is the chess." She went back to the kitchen and started fussing at the stove, preparing something.

Joshua's grandfather moved his bishop, very slowly. "Aha! There! I'm sorry for you!" he said in a deep voice that seemed at odds with his fragile body and shaky hands. "Check!"

"Oh, brother!" said Joshua, with exaggerated fear. "What's the man doing to me!"

"You'll find out. It's an old trap." His grandfather turned toward Karen. "I'm eighty-three years old, and I can still beat the pants off this friend of yours." He turned back to Joshua. "You say you beat Klein last Saturday?"

"Well, he blundered."

"He would. . . . So you can beat Klein, and I can beat you. See? Very simple. One and one is two. . . . Karen? Nice name. Karen. . . . This is my grandson."

"I know."

"He's a sweet kid. Am I right?"

"Oh, right!"

"Come on, Granpa," said Joshua, studying the board.

"A sweet kid . . . until he gets behind a chessboard. Have you ever seen him in a tournament? Vicious. Vicious. Worse than I ever was. . . . Am I right, Joshua? Hah?"

"Right, right. . . ."

He certainly didn't seem vicious now, thought Karen. Or ever. Sweet was a much better word. He *was* sweet.

"OK, I'll push the pawn," said Joshua. "You'll have to move that bishop now. I don't think I see the trap."

"Wait! You'll find out. Patience, patience. Rome wasn't built in a day. . . . Vicious, yes. Karen? You're Karen, yes?"

"Yes."

"A beautiful name. . . . Let me see. I'll bring out the rook." He started to lift his rook, but Joshua put his hand gently on his grandfather's. "Granpa, wait a second."

93

Even Karen could see that Joshua's pawn could take the bishop on the next move. It would be a real blunder. Yet Joshua had said his grandfather had been a champion chess player in his day. A grandmaster, he'd said. It was so sad . . .

"You wanted to move the bishop, Granpa, right? I'm sorry, I think I got you all mixed up. . . ."

"Of course. The bishop. We'll pull back. So!"

"OK. I'll—hmm—I'll move the old king knight."

"Ahh . . . let me see. Now I'll move my rook."

"Uh, wait a second, Granpa. With that knight, I've got one piece more than you on your pawn, I think . . . right?"

"Yes, yes, yes. Good, good. I'll come with my knight first. Why not? Good."

It was clear to Karen that Joshua's grandfather could scarcely recognize a present danger, let alone plan moves ahead. Joshua was virtually playing for him and, what was more, was slowly but surely letting him win. He was terrific, Joshua! Not like her father, who took every loss, no matter how trivial, as a personal disaster.

Joshua moved a piece on the chessboard, then looked toward Karen squatting on the floor. He shrugged as if to say he was losing, then smiled at her.

She wanted to hug him. He was beautiful. Beautiful. Definitely!

Joshua's grandmother came in from the kitchen carrying a platter of blintzes, hot little cylinders of dough with fillings of strawberry jam and cheese. "Time for some strength for the chess players and the audience," she said.

"Oh, that smells good," said Karen.

"Eat and enjoy. My favorite words," his grandmother said.

"Thank you. They look great," said Karen, gingerly taking one of the blintzes.

"Joshua," his grandmother said, "I think Granpa maybe has had enough of chess today. He gets very tired, yes?" She nodded firmly so that Joshua could see she'd meant it seriously.

"Oh, right," said Joshua. "I think you've won it already, Granpa; you could blitz me whenever you want to. I concede." Joshua laid his king down on the board.

"You might yet win. . . ."

"I don't think so. My position is terrible," said Joshua.

"Ahh . . . yes, yes . . . nice game. . . . Shake."

Joshua took his grandfather's hand in his and carefully shook it.

"Yes. . . ." His grandfather seemed to be staring past the walls of the room. "I remember a game like this . . . 1934, Zurich. Before Hitler. You could still play tournament chess in Europe. Too much pawn pushing. I lost to Klein then. Amazing. I can still remember that final position . . . but I can't remember what I did yesterday. Absolutely amazing—I can even remember things my own grandfather told me seventy years ago. . . . Seventy years . . ." He rubbed his face with a shaky hand, lost in thought. After a pause, he continued. "He was very old when I was a little boy, my grandfather. He was as old then as I am now . . . . I remember the day he told me something *his* grandfather had told *him*, long ago, when he himself was a little kid. . . . Yes . . . yes . . . What was I getting at?"

"About your grandfather telling you about *his* grandfather," said Joshua. "Karen, listen to this. It's an incredible story. My grandfather's favorite."

"Yes, yes. . . . Let me see—my own grandfather told me that *his* grandfather heard, when he was a little boy—this was in old-time Bavaria—a town crier. They still had town criers then. Calling the news, with a bell, that England had lost. England had lost. England was defeated . . . see? From my grandfather's grandfather to me . . . word of mouth. England lost the war . . . see?"

"You left something out, Granpa. Which war was it?"

"The American Revolution. Amazing. From my grandfather's grandfather to me . . . and me to you. . . . Amazing." He turned toward Karen. "Did you like that story?"

"I loved it! I wish Lori—I wish a friend of mine could have been here. She loves things like that. I'll tell her."

Joshua wished Lori were there, too. She would like his grandparents; he was sure of it. Was she OK? Karen had said Lori was still asleep when she'd phoned earlier.

"Everybody should talk to the old people," his grandfather continued. "Ask us. We have stories, stories . . . better than history books . . . . Ask me anything. I remember seventy-five years ago better than this morning."

"Well . . ." Karen hesitated. "Was it better to be a kid seventy-five years ago? Compared to now?"

"As long as you didn't get sick. Much better. . . . Sick was bad. The doctors didn't know anything then. Nothing. . . . But if you didn't get too sick, much better then. . . . When we played, we were like gods, because we made up a whole world. From sticks. From dirt. From string. From rain, even. Wind. Even the stars— you could see the stars then, oh yes. . . . From the stars. From the brook outside my town. We made up a world. . . . Now you go to the movies. You turn on TV. You play with all those electronic games. *They* make up the world for you. . . . It was much better then. I feel sorry for you both. Unless you got sick. Sick was bad. . . . Amazing. The American Revolution . . ."

His grandfather's robe had slipped, but his grandmother immediately adjusted it, smoothing it as if it were a blanket. "Well, well," she said, "there's other things. Joshua couldn't have visited us so easy then. It would be a day each way from New Jersey then. Now we have busses, trains, airplanes—"

"Yes," his grandfather cut in, "and also bombs, missiles, submarines."

"Right," said Karen softly.

"We had wars back then, too," his grandmother said.

"Not like now . . . not like now. . . ." His grandfather hitched himself forward in his chair. "Now even

97

the chess isn't good anymore. Even the chess. No more gentlemen. No more. They play like lunatics. The care, the poetry in the chess . . . no more. Like lunatics. Amazing. . . . I feel sorry for you both. . . ."

"We're OK, Granpa. We really are," said Joshua, wondering if they actually were.

"That's what it is today. . . . Your mother doesn't even know how to cook. She's my daughter, but she can't cook. A good heart, yes; she loves you, yes. But look how skinny you are. She can't cook."

Joshua noticed how Karen was struggling to contain herself and not say something. About stereotyping of women, no doubt. She'd said it often enough in history class. "Come on, Granpa: I'm skinny because you're skinny. It runs in the family. Look at Granma."

"Maybe . . . maybe . . . but she can't even boil an egg."

"I think we've got to go. My match is at twelve-thirty." Please, he thought. Karen, don't make a speech. Please . . .

"Thank you for all the good stuff," said Karen. "The tea and cake and those terrific hot things—"

"Blintzes," said his grandmother.

"Right. And for your terrific story about the Revolution."

"Yes. Amazing . . . Karen . . . Karen?"

"Yes."

"Can you cook?"

"Not too well. But I—I look at the stars sometimes.

Just like you said *you* did. How's that? I go into my backyard with my friend, Lori, and we stargaze."

"Ah. That's good. That's good. . . . I hope I'll meet you again."

"Me too."

As everyone said good-bye and Joshua's grandmother kissed him, his grandfather took something from his pocket and held it out shakily toward Karen.

"Please . . . this is for you . . . Karen."

"Oh, I can't take that from—"

"Please."

"Oh . . . thank you." It was a tiny compass, no larger than a dime.

"That's so you can find the North Star. Always you have to find first the North Star. . . . This compass is seventy-years old."

"Oh, I can't!"

"It's yours. I can't look at the stars anymore. Look with Joshua."

"Thank you so much. We will."

"Yes . . . better than TV. Much better. . . ."

After another round of good-byes, Joshua and Karen walked down the tiled hallway to the elevator. As they waited for the elevator to come up from the ground floor, Karen tried to give the compass to Joshua.

"No, he gave it to you," said Joshua.

"But he's your grandfather. You should have it."

"That's OK. He's given me all sorts of stuff. I've got a hundred-year-old chess set. It was his father's. I'll show it to you. . . . Karen? Thanks a lot."

"For what?"

"For not—you know—getting all excited about that cooking stuff. He's still pretty old-fashioned."

"I know. Come on, Josh! What do you think I am! You let him win. Why can't *I* let him win? Besides, I like him. And your grandmother, too. I wish they were mine."

"Hey . . . you're—you're great!"

In the elevator, he suddenly held her and tried to kiss her. She laughed, and his teeth struck her teeth with an audible click. Which made them laugh all the way out to the lobby.

14

Lori lay in bed late that Saturday morning, between sleep and waking, trying to hold on to the sleep. Something had shifted in her life; the day ahead seemed like an ocean without land. She imagined the bed was a life raft. She clutched the edge of the mattress and pressed her head down into her pillow. Her tongue felt so dry. Visions of sailors dying of thirst. That poem from English class, *The Rime of the Ancient Mariner*.

The bed was safe. The pillow, the blanket, the squeaky springs. The little tear at the edge of the pale-yellow sheet.

Karen would never be all hers again, not ever. She should hate Joshua. If only he were Mark. But he wasn't;

he was himself, and she loved him, and Karen was gone. Was gone, for all her words. And she, Lori, would always be a third wheel now.

The commotion of life from downstairs—a TV speaking to itself, her sister calling to her mother—finally roused her. Lori sat up and shook her head. Her headache was gone. She put her hand in front of her face, exhaled, and sniffed her breath. No smell of scotch. All right! She would get up. And go somewhere. Anywhere. For the day.

She dressed quickly, put her drawing material into her backpack, took the last of the mints, then went downstairs to the kitchen. Her sister, Lisa, was sitting at the table putting on clear nail polish.

"Karen called twice," said Lisa. "She kept asking me how you were, and I kept saying you were sleeping. She said to let you sleep and she'll call you tonight, after she gets back from New York. End of message. Bleep!"

"Thanks," said Lori. "Why don't you paint your nails purple?"

"Very funny. How was the dance?" asked Lisa.

"OK. . . . Do we have any cheese in the refrigerator?"

"I don't know. . . . Tell me about the dance!"

"It was—fabulous! Just *awesome*!" said Lori, with mock exaggeration. She tossed a banana, a pear, and a chunk of Swiss cheese into her backpack.

"Come on! Really! Tell me!"

"Later." Lori called to her mother in the living room,

102

"Mom! I'm biking to Jockey Hollow. To do some drawing. I'll be home around five."

"That's too far, Lori!" her mother called back. "How was the dance? You looked sick last night."

"It was *fabulous*! I'm going! So long!"

"Can I come?" asked Lisa.

"No," said Lori.

"Why not?" her sister asked automatically.

Her mother was at the kitchen door now. "Lori, I've just told you. It's much too far to bike there alone. Go with Karen."

"So long," said Lori, brushing past her mother. "I'll see you at five."

"Lori!"

But she was gone. She raced up the driveway and into the street on her bicycle, pedaling furiously to get out of earshot. As she turned the corner, she slowed up.

The same houses. White, green, brown. Everyone doing what they were supposed to do. Like little kids playing at being grown-ups. The make-believe mailman in his red, white, and blue make-believe mail truck. The husbands spreading lime and fertilizer, all make-believe, on their make-believe lawns. And did they make make-believe love at night to their make-believe wives to have make-believe children? Is that what Karen and Joshua really wanted: to become make-believe people?

Why did she feel so mean? They had the right to go to New York City and do whatever they liked. They had the right, no matter what she, Lori, felt. They did!

103

She turned onto Route 53 and pedaled south toward Morris Plains. She had to bike carefully; the road had no shoulder. For a fleeting second she wished a car would hit her. She pictured herself in the hospital, everyone around her bed, Karen and Joshua, Lisa, her mother and father, everyone. She would almost die, but not quite. She would know they were there even though she was unconscious. . . .

She pedaled through Morris Plains and turned west at the Square in Morristown. The Square was crowded that Saturday; everyone shopping for summer things. All make-believe. She had always loved the block-square park at Christmas, with its gigantic wooden hobby horses and wooden soldiers and Santa's house full of toys. That had always seemed real to her: the trees all decorated, the hidden speakers with Christmas carols that seemed to descend from the sky. But everything was make-believe now, in the Saturday-morning sunlight.

She pedaled down the long road into Jockey Hollow, past the armory, past the last houses, into the woods. The trees overarched the road; the split-rail fence at one side rose and fell and rose again with the rise and fall of the hillocks. Now the biking was delicious. The trees held the light in green baskets. A wood thrush sounded. Another. Then a mockingbird, somewhere, took over the music.

At the apple orchard, she searched deep into the woods and spotted one, two deer. She'd biked down this road many times with Karen, and every spring they'd seen deer, sometimes in the woods, sometimes in the orchard, once crossing the road in front of them.

They could bike here sometime and have a picnic, all three of them. At a picnic, maybe she wouldn't be a third wheel. Yes, she would suggest it. . . . She felt tense, suddenly. The orchard. That shade, there. Those ancient apple trees. It was her blue-green place! She'd never made the connection before. . . . No, they couldn't have a picnic here! Only alone, with herself, inside. It was too special here.

She stopped and chained her bike to one of the posts of the wooden fence, then climbed over the fence and sat at the edge of the field. From her backpack she took out a pad and some charcoal pencils. She decided to sketch the nearest tree and put a deer in the picture. Or a person. Or two people. . . .

She worked slowly, closing her eyes, looking, then closing her eyes again to draw what she saw within. She sketched the apple tree with its twisted branches like Medusa's hair. The edge of the fence. Then Joshua. And Karen. Joshua and Karen lying in each other's arms on the grass, naked. She drew and felt light-headed; her hand was shaking slightly. She tried to draw herself with them. Behind them—she erased—in front—no—at the side—no. The drawing was a dark smear of lines and blurs. She crumpled it, threw it into her backpack, and tried another. Joshua and Karen, standing. What was she doing! She didn't care; she would draw everything! Let it be obscene. But it wasn't. It wasn't. It was beautiful! Beautiful! She wished the drawing could come to life, that she could enter it, become intertwined with them, as one intertwines one's fingers. If she only could. If only . . . she rubbed herself, and wished, and rubbed again, until she closed her eyes, finally, and disappeared for a moment into pure feeling . . . .

There were people coming down the field. A man and woman, walking slowly, a dog before them. Lori carefully folded the drawing over and over to form a small packet, then dug into the ground before her. She took the small bundle of folded paper and kissed it gently, then put it into the ground and covered it with dark earth.

She sat quietly until the couple and their dog passed by, held back a moment, then let herself cry, silently, into the blinding spring sun.

15

Karen hadn't expected the Metropolitan Chess Club to be so rich-looking. The deep red carpeting and wood-paneled walls, the paintings and trophies, the heavy oak tables with inlaid chessboards, all reminded her of a British club she'd seen in a James Bond movie.

The long main room was crowded with chess players and onlookers, yet the mood appeared hushed. Only the faces of the players betrayed the tension. . . . No, not quite a British club, Karen decided; more like a posh gambling casino with millions at stake.

Joshua sat at one of the chess tables, his fingertips poised on the edge as if he were about to spring at his opponent, Tom Benziger. Joshua had introduced Benziger to Karen earlier, but she'd thought he'd seemed cool, almost unfriendly. Not for Lori, Karen had thought.

As the match progressed, Benziger appeared to grow more and more relaxed, almost bored, with his feet stretched out under the table. Not like Joshua, who sat frowning as he bit his lip continuously. Was he losing?

It all seemed so strange to Karen: the double clocks at every table for timing the moves, the score pads, the huge wooden chess pieces. And everyone playing or watching so intently, in absolute silence, boys younger than Joshua, men as old as his grandfather. And women in a match of their own. Why had they been segregated? But no, there *were* a few women playing the men. Strange.

And they made their moves so slowly. How long could you think about one little move? Karen wandered from table to table, always coming back to Joshua's game. He looked so grim. So angry. Vicious, his grandfather had said. He didn't even notice that she was there.

That was how her father had played tennis, as if nothing else in the world mattered. She'd gone down to the courts with him to watch when she was younger, but he'd played as if she didn't exist. Had played like a maniac. And after a time she'd stopped going.

And Joshua, wasn't he doing the same thing? Look at him scowling! The Joshua she cared about, the Joshua who let his grandfather win, that Joshua seemed gone completely.

She walked out to the street to get away for a while. The sun had burned off the haze, and Madison Avenue

108

was festive with spring colors. She studied the paintings in the windows of the art galleries and looked at the latest fashions in the little boutiques. Everything seemed artificial. The modern paintings were so bloodless, the passersby so phony in their expensive outfits, designed for one season or less. It was all a game, a hype. Everybody trying to be chic. Like her father—why was she thinking about him so much?—and that phony Diane living with him. Oh, God, she hoped she wouldn't meet him in the street; his new apartment was only a few blocks away.

She had a sudden wild thought of visiting him, in spite of everything. Her mother had been urging her, almost begging her, to give it a chance. To visit him again. Well, maybe she would. With Joshua. Or with Joshua and Lori, both. Safety in numbers. Her father had always liked Lori. Maybe next week. Good idea.

Was that her father on the next block? . . . No, someone else. . . . She was surprised to find herself vaguely disappointed. What was going on? Incredible. After all she'd said and felt, how could she want to accidentally meet him? . . . Maybe Joshua could figure that one out. He was into psychology, wasn't he?

She delayed returning to the chess club as long as possible, stopping for a peach-apricot ice-cream cone and licking it round and round, as slowly as she could. Why did she always have to eat, eat, eat, whenever she was upset? . . .

She watched a trio playing classical music in front of the Whitney Museum. They announced each piece:

Scarlatti, Bach, Saint-Saëns. Complex, delicate inter-lacings. Joshua should be here with her, listening, being a part of the scene instead of bending over that stupid chess game, biting his lips.

This trio was wonderful; they seemed to love the music, the listening crowd, the very day itself. Lori was like that when she was at her best. Karen suddenly wondered if she should call Lori long distance. . . . What an idea! Yes!

She tossed a coin into the open cello case, next to the other bills and coins, threw the remnant of her ice-cream cone into a wastebasket, and headed for a phone.

Lori's mother answered, after what seemed like end-less rings. "She's out. She went biking. To Jockey Hol-low. . . ."

"Oh. Could you tell her, when she gets back, that I'll call her tonight?" asked Karen.

"Yes, but Karen, before you hang up . . . what hap-pened at that dance? She came home last night and went right to the bathroom; I think she threw up. And not a word from her. She just looked right past me, like usual. Karen, what happened?"

"Nothing really happened, Mrs. Lindstrom. . . . She might have eaten some junk. I felt a little sick too."

"You too? Oh, that's good. I don't mean *good*, but at least she wasn't doing something . . . wrong."

"Oh, definitely," said Karen into the phone, "the food they had there was real gar-baage."

"Oh . . . well, why did you let her eat such stuff?"

110

Oh, no, thought Karen. There she goes again, acting like Lori's a five-year-old or feebleminded, and I'm her nurse. "Well, I ate it *too*," she said.

"Oh. Well, I'm relieved. You hear so much about drugs . . . But of course, you would never let her touch anything."

"Of course not, Mrs. Lindstrom! But I'm not with her every second! You know, if you're so worried about her . . . maybe you should get her some—some counseling, or something." There; she'd said it! It was easier on the phone, without having to see Mrs. Lindstrom's face.

"Karen, what do you mean?"

"Counseling. Help. I don't know. I've been sort of worried about her, too . . . you know?"

"I'm not worried at all! She's perfectly fine. I just asked because she threw up."

Oh, great, thought Karen. She's backing off! Well, I'm going to tell it to her straight.

"Well," said Karen, "I think she should be seeing a psychologist, Mrs. Lindstrom. I really do."

"Why should she?" said Mrs. Lindstrom. "What's wrong with her? Did Lori tell you to say that?"

"No. *I'm* saying it. I'm sorry, but I've got to. It's easier over the phone. And I—"

"You have no right to lecture at me, Karen! On the phone or anyplace else! I know you care about Lori. I know you care. But we're her parents, and I think we still know what's best. There's nothing wrong with her.

She's just artistic. Just very artistic. She has such an imagination."

"Oh, brother. You always say she's artistic, Mrs. Lindstrom, whenever anything happens."

"She *is* artistic! Why are you going on and on about this?" Suddenly, strangely, it was almost Lori's voice, even to the edge of tears.

"OK! OK!" said Karen. "I'm sorry! I'm sorry! It's hopeless! I'm sorry!"

A series of clicks ratcheted over the phone, then a man's unctuous voice said, "Eighty cents. Please deposit eighty cents for the next three minutes."

"Where *are* you, Karen?"

"I'm in New York right now. And I don't have any more coins. I have to hang up. I'll call Lori tonight. Good-bye."

"Good-bye, Karen."

The phone hummed as the line disconnected. Well, she'd finally done it! She'd finally talked to Mrs. Lindstrom about Lori. On a long-distance phone call to boot. But the distance had somehow made it easier. Good! Let it cook in her brain.

As Karen walked back toward the chess club, she was tempted to buy another ice cream. Strawberry-lime. Wild! What could *that* combination taste like? But she resisted. She was just feeling uptight about that phone call, and about Joshua, and about Lori, and about everything.

After the bright busy avenue, the long room full of chess players and viewers seemed to belong to a science-fiction movie. The room of the living dead. Unreal. But there were fragments of conversation now. Some of the games had ended. And wasn't that coffee she smelled?

There was a large group around Joshua's table. He still sat tensely at the edge of his chair, and he was still frowning, but his face looked less desperate. Tom Benziger was sitting upright, concentrating. There were only a few pieces left on the board: rooks, some pawns, a knight, a bishop, and the kings, each in a corner.

Benziger moved a pawn one square and hit his chess clock. With almost no pause, Joshua moved a corresponding pawn and pressed his chess clock, too. He nodded to himself, as if confirming a plan that was working.

Benziger moved his rook; Joshua mirrored the move with *his* rook. Benziger shrugged, then, breaking the silence, said, "Well, screw this! We could do this all day. I've got better ways to waste an afternoon. Offer you a draw, Freeman."

"Accept," said Joshua.

"You pulled the game out, Freeman," said Benziger. "You're getting to actually play chess. Hot stuff."

Joshua frowned at the condescension while they shook hands, limply, over the game. Standing at the periphery of the group, Karen noticed that Joshua was still biting his lip. He'd wanted to win. A draw hadn't been good enough. He had to win!

Joshua worked his way through the knot of onlookers toward Karen. The club secretary, Edelbaum, took Joshua's score sheet, and someone else patted him on the back. "Tough fight," said the man. "Nice going."

"Thanks," Joshua answered without conviction. He stood in front of Karen, his face still fixed in a dull frown. "I didn't win," he said flatly.

"So what?" she said. "So you didn't win! What does that do, make you into a wimp?"

"Yes! Let's get out of here!"

"I can't wait!"

They walked down Madison Avenue for blocks without speaking. Joshua's face was sullen; he scarcely looked up. What was wrong with him? wondered Karen. It was just a stupid *game*! Good grief!

"Let's go over to Central Park awhile," she said suddenly.

"Don't you want to get something to eat?" asked Joshua, still sullen.

"No! I want to talk!"

"OK. But why are you angry?"

"I'm not angry!"

They sat on a bench in the zoo, facing the seals sunning on their concrete steps. Their sleek coats shone darkly. Every so often, a seal would lift its head and sniff the air, hoping for fish.

"So what do you want to talk about?" Joshua asked glumly.

"You!"

"Me? Oh. OK." Joshua stared at the seals.

"Do you know what you look like when you play chess? I mean in a tournament?"

"I don't know. My grandfather said vicious, right?"

114

"You—you look so angry, as if you hated the person you're playing and everybody in the world. You look mean. Actually mean. If I saw you for the first time playing chess like that, I—I'd never want to go out with you."

"Well, I was losing. I just barely pulled a draw."

"I don't care about that. I care about *you*. It's just a game! How can you let a game turn you into a—a yich person like that? It's like Jekyll and Hyde. I don't remember which was the bad one, but that's what you became!"

"Maybe it's only a game to you," said Joshua, "but it happens to be my life!"

"Oh, bull! You sound like some kind of Shakespearean actor. The theatuh is my life! It's just a game! Why not become an expert on some video game? Then you could say: Star Battles is my life!"

Joshua felt the burning anger in him moving toward tears. She had no right! He hadn't done anything to her. She had no right!

"I—I don't tell you want to do with your—with your stickers on magazines and your antinuke buttons and—"

"Those things are important! We could all be blown to dust any day by an H-bomb! How can you compare that to a game! And do you know who does all that stuff? Who does the H-bombs? People who think they have to win. Who think they have to—have to . . . Oh shit!" She bit her lip not to cry.

"Come on! That's crazy!" he pleaded. "Chess is a game of—of gentlemen—"

115

"Not the way *you* play! You make it—you make it ugly! It's like you're on drugs. That's it. It's like a drug. And you can't kick the habit."

"Oh, this is great!" said Joshua. "Now I've got my mother and father *and* you against me! Just great. . . ."

They sat for minutes, neither saying a word, watching the seals, dully. Joshua felt frozen in place; if he walked away, she'd probably never speak to him again. But she had no right! Not even his parents had attacked him like that. They'd tried to reason with him; it was a matter of making a living, of not having endless disappointments trying to become a grandmaster.

But could she be right? Hadn't he had plenty of doubts himself? Maybe chess *was* a drug. Maybe he had to get lost in it; lost in a chess world where he could be powerful and brilliant and admired. Admired by other chess maniacs, at least. He'd often felt at the end of a difficult game as if he'd just come out of an absorbing movie, back into the real world. And just as with the movie, the real world was a letdown. A drag. Wasn't that what the psychology books said about the feeling when you came off drugs?

Karen sighed and looked at Joshua. "Josh, I'm—I'm sorry for shouting at you. I really am. Josh, I—I'm sorry. It's that I don't want to lose you; the you I like. Maybe I'm crazy. I want you to be that way, always. Gentle. Nice. Do you know what I mean? Josh?"

"Nobody's that simple. Nobody's just sugar and spice. . . . Karen, I understand what you're saying. I

116

do. I'll think about it, OK? I will. I wonder myself. Plenty. What I'm doing with my life . . ."

"That's good," said Karen. "Because I think you could be a *great* psychologist! Or anything! You could really *help* people. You could do so much!"

Joshua shook his head skeptically. "I don't know . . . maybe . . . I know I wish I could help Lori—"

"That's what I mean!"

"I don't know. . . . I've got to think."

Karen stretched her arms in relief. "I guess we've had our first real fight. You know what they say, don't you?"

"No. What?"

"You don't really have a relationship—oh, how I hate that word—if you don't go through your first fight."

"Oh, right. . . . So I guess now we have a relationship," said Joshua.

"Isn't it disgusting?"

"Sickening. We might as well get married."

Karen laughed. "Next year."

"But by next year we're supposed to be divorced."

"Oh . . ." Her expression darkened.

Joshua drew in his breath. Why was he always saying boneheaded things like that! Her parents *were* divorced.

"I'm sorry. That wasn't funny," he said.

"That's OK. It's true. That's America, right? . . . You know, I may visit my father next weekend. He lives near here."

"Hey," said Joshua, "we could come into the city

117

together again. My last game's next Saturday. Do you want to?"

"Sure. But I want to ask Lori, too. OK?"

"OK."

"And I don't want to watch you play chess."

"OK. But I promise to smile during the whole match, like this. See?" He twisted his mouth into a comic smile.

"No way. . . . I don't know, Josh. Maybe it's because of my father, but this chess thing has really hit a nerve. . . . I guess I have to do some thinking, too. . . . Come on! Let's go eat, OK?"

"You better believe. I'm starving."

As they strolled out of the park, Joshua hesitated, then put his arm around Karen. He felt awkward doing it; he wondered if he was still a little angry at her. Well, maybe he should be. She'd acted as if playing chess made him evil; she'd actually said it with that Jekyll and Hyde stuff. Why couldn't she just leave him alone? Why couldn't she be a little more laid back, a little more spaced out, like Lori?

He suddenly pictured himself walking with his arm around Lori. Lori again. What was going on?

Karen put her arm around him, too, and kissed him on his cheek as they walked. A let's-have-peace kiss. He tried to resist, but after a moment she kissed him again, playfully. His defenses collapsed. He turned toward her and they kissed, walking. Again their teeth clashed, and again they laughed. And she was there, returned, as if nothing had happened, the warm Karen, the Karen *he* liked.

118

16

Joshua slept fitfully Saturday night, dreaming of chess openings and barking dogs. He awoke again and again. Karen was in one of the dreams; she was whispering in his ear, whispering moves in chess notation: e-4, e-5; Nf-3, Nf-6; N takes at e-5. . . . Suddenly there were bombs blasting; H-bombs, yellow and red, like Fourth of July fireworks, crackling overhead.

He woke up Sunday morning feeling exhausted and slightly dizzy. How was he going to play tournament chess today? He felt so tired.

And at breakfast his parents didn't make matters any easier. "Look, Joshua," his father said, "you can't keep this up. New York, home. New York, home. It's lunacy.

What do I have to do to make you get some sense? When do you do any homework?"

"I'll do it tonight," said Joshua sullenly.

"Tonight. It's always tonight. Or better still, tomorrow. I have a son with an IQ that says he's brilliant, he ought to be first in his class, and he gets a sixty-three in—what? What was the sixty-three in, Sylvia?"

His mother sighed with exasperation. "If you don't know, why ask me! Ask *him*! . . . It was in French."

"I hate French!" said Joshua. "Who needs French?"

"Who needs *chess*?" his father answered.

"I do!" Oh, not again, he thought. First Karen, now them! They're driving me nuts!

"You know, Joshua, you read all those psychology books," his mother said, "and you're not exactly a dope. Can't you see what this chess can do to you? Look at Granpa. He has no pension, no money put away, nothing. They have a little Social Security because, thank God, Granma was able to work here and there. Do you know who helps support them now? Because my sister can't. Your terrible father, that's who. Your father supports his in-laws. How's that! That's what chess did for Granpa. Can you imagine what kind of humiliation this is for him? He was always so proud."

"I think Granpa is fine!" said Joshua, feeling a dull lump inside. If he couldn't keep his breakfast down, he'd never be able to play today. . . . Was his grandfather humiliated? Joshua wondered whether he saw everything that was going on. . . . "He's fine," Joshua repeated, without conviction.

120

"Fine? Crippled? Beat down? That's fine? Joshua, what are you telling me? I'm trying to explain something and—"

"OK! But I'm not Granpa! And when I'm sixteen, I'm quitting school and playing chess full time even if I have to live in a flophouse!" Why was he so angry? Was he shouting at them this morning because he hadn't shouted at Karen yesterday? Or was he feeling guilty about his grandfather? But guilty for what? No analyzing! Oh, what a Sunday this was going to be!

His father placed his knife and fork carefully on his plate, then stared directly at Joshua. "Joshua, when you're of legal age—and I think it's eighteen in New Jersey, but I could be wrong—when you're of legal age, *no* one can tell you what to do. But right at this moment I happen to be your father, and this lady over here happens to be your mother, and we are, by law, mind you, supposed to look out for your welfare. OK? That's what we're trying to do. You look like you're about to cave in from all this chess, and running back and forth into New York, and seeing this girl. It's too much. Something has to give. Do I make myself clear?"

"Yes! Yes!"

"That's all. Eat your breakfast. Your mother's made these pancakes with all natural ingredients; it's delicious. I think. At least it's healthy. I think. . . ."

His father was trying to calm things with humor. Let it be, thought Joshua. "These pancakes *are* good, Mom . . . I think."

"Then eat, wise guy!" she said.

121

He noticed the time on the digital clock above the refrigerator: 8:16. "Oh boy!" he said. "I've got to go! I'll do some homework on the bus. Could you make me a chicken sandwich, while I get my books? Please?"

"Fine!" said his mother. "But who's going to make you chicken sandwiches when you go to live in a flop-house, may I ask?"

"*You* will. You'll probably mail them to me, with vitamin pills."

"Beautiful. Always the wise answer," his mother said. "I probably would, at that. . . ."

The day seemed endless to Joshua. French and algebra on the bus to Manhattan. Then the subway to the chess club, with more French on the subway. Then the tournament. His neck and back ached from tension. The first game was the tough one; he drew again. There was an hour's break between games; he sat at the back of the club doing algebra problems. His second opponent was a mercifully weak player; he didn't really belong in a tournament of this caliber. Joshua won in only twenty-eight moves. An hour saved. And he remained in third place in the tournament, though he was covered with sweat from the sheer effort of concentrating. It had never seemed this difficult before.

On the bus back to New Jersey, he opened his French text, started conjugating *pouvoir*, then fell asleep. He awoke abruptly in Boonton, one stop before his. The bus growled along the main avenue of Lake Hills, past familiar shops, to the residential area, heavy with trees.

So different and distant from the steel and concrete of New York.

He tried to look wide awake and full of energy as he walked into the living room. They were there, both his mother and father, reading the Sunday papers with their after-dinner coffee.

"How did you make out?" his father asked.

"I got one and a half points. I'm still in third place."

"That sounds pretty good."

"Pretty good? Dad, the United States champion is in this tournament! And the U.S. Junior Champion! And two ex-grandmasters! And I'm in *third place*! And that's just pretty good? Bob Kim's father would have been as proud as hell!"

His mother slammed her paper onto the coffee table. "Listen, Joshua!" she said. "We're not having another round of this tonight. Enough is enough! I've heard third places from your grandfather all my life, and first places, and second places, and last places. We don't care *what* place you're in. Only *you* care what place you're in."

"That's obvious!" said Joshua, heading for his room.

He sat on his bed and stared at the chess sets on his desk. Maybe they were right, all of them. Maybe it really was crazy. The sleep on the bus had helped clear his head. He studied the chess sets surgically. Why did he need the game so much? Why did he need to go back into the world of chess all the time as if he were Alice going through the looking glass? What was wrong with the world of Lake Hills, New Jersey?

123

In that world he was just a skinny teenager who everybody thought was weird, except Karen and Lori, maybe. A skinny teenager who couldn't even kiss right, who went out with one girl yet couldn't help suddenly thinking about another, who was all messed up and didn't know what was going on in his body or his brain. Things had never seemed this complicated before. Chess had been easy compared to this. This was all feeling. You couldn't *think* feelings. He could try, but it wouldn't really work. If only he had the time, he could reread some of those psychology books on his shelf. Maybe that would help. But he *didn't* have the time. He didn't even have time to sleep.

Next Saturday he'd have to face John Valerian, the U.S. Champion. One short week to study Valerian's past games. Forget about sleep.

17

By Tuesday evening Joshua's left eyelid had started to twitch from eyestrain and tension. It had happened before, always his left upper eyelid, a small fluttering weak spot. A warning to take it easy.

But he continued to study during every free moment away from Karen: chess and French, French and chess. He began mumbling moves to himself in pidgin French, "Pawn *à roi quatre*." And as he pondered John Valerian's use of the Gruenfeld Defense, he found himself automatically conjugating infinitives ending in *oir*: *pouvoir, savoir, vouloir*. Why had he ever taken French? Karen couldn't help him with it; she was taking Spanish. No one could help him; he was a language imbecile. Unless chess could be considered a language.

He lived and breathed Valerian all week. In game after game, Joshua saw the same pattern: orderliness, care, no dramatic moves. But Valerian clamped onto an opponent's least error like a bulldog and wouldn't let go until the slight misjudgment grew into a broken pawn structure, a ripped-open defense, a catastrophe.

By Wednesday the eye twitch had grown worse; it bothered him constantly during biology class. Maybe he needed glasses. Or twenty-four hours of solid sleep.

As he walked with Karen and Lori to Lori's math class, Karen suggested they all come over to her house that evening. Joshua leaped at the idea; it would be a perfect escape from French and chess for one night. But Lori said she couldn't make it.

"Come on," said Karen. "We could do our star tracking, Lori. We'll show Josh that we're experts at something too. Lor, you know that little compass Josh's grandfather gave me—the one I showed you? It reminded me: we haven't done the stars for a long time."

"I've got too much homework," said Lori. "You and Josh go ahead." No more third wheel. Not ever.

"But you're the only one who can ever find the Pleiades. Come on, Lori. Let's make sure the universe is still in one piece."

"No . . . I don't think so . . ." Lori said listlessly.

"OK. I give up. . . . But you *are* coming into New York with us Saturday, aren't you?"

"Uh-huh . . . if the universe is still in one piece by then. . . ." Lori moved her fingers in a little good-bye wave, then slipped past Joshua and Karen into her classroom.

"OK, let's go to lunch, Josh," said Karen. "I'll cut my study period again. . . . God, I wish Lori would snap out of it. What's wrong with her?"

"Maybe I'm in the way," said Joshua over the din, as they walked down the main corridor toward the cafeteria. "If you've always done that stargazing alone with her, maybe she thinks I'm butting in."

"But you're not. She could come if she wanted to. . . . Anyway, it could be fun, just you and me and the stars. Doesn't it sound romantic?"

"Definitely. We could play old Bing Crosby records," said Joshua. "And maybe I can find a mandolin someplace. How does that sound?"

"Devastating. But romantic or not, this is serious star studies, right? Serious stuff. No fooling around."

"OK. I'll take a cold shower first."

"Josh! That's gross! You're beginning to sound like those nitwits at the burger joint."

"Really? Maybe it's about time."

"You do that, and I'll start going to the mall to shop for three hours to find the exact right shade of nail polish. Like Lori's kid sister."

"OK!" said Joshua. "This is as good a time as any! I've been meaning to have a serious talk with you about that nail polish you've been using. It's—well, it's *gross*, Karen!"

"But I don't use any nail— OK, Josh. Very funny."

127

They sat at their usual corner table in the cafeteria, near the tray-return window. Their table was littered with empty milk containers, fragments of sandwiches, and a pile of dishes.

"Talk about gross," said Karen, as she pushed everything to one end. "That stuff must be from yesterday."

"I brought my lunch today," said Joshua. "A liverwurst sandwich with onions and mayo. Want some?"

"That's grosser! You know, it's so awful, it sounds perversely tempting. OK, Josh. I'll trade you half of my tuna salad sandwich for half of your belch special."

As they ate their sandwiches, Joshua took his small pocket chess set out and put it on the table. "OK," he said, "how about the weirdos doing their thing again? I've got the chess set today."

Karen put her sandwich down. "Oh, no. I've become allergic to chess. I have!"

"But this is just for fun—"

"Josh, please! In fact, you were going to think about chess and about helping people and all. Remember?"

"I will, but give me a break! I've got one more week of this tournament. Don't psych me out, Karen. Let me finish what I started."

"OK, I'll get off your case. But don't worry, Josh. I'll hound you again. Karen the Crank never stops. . . ."

Why couldn't she let it be? he wondered. What if he told her he'd *never* quit playing? What would she do? Would she stop going out with him? He knew deep within that he was afraid to test it. Maybe he'd never have to; maybe he *would* decide to quit. . . . Or was he just kidding himself?

That evening, stretched out on a blanket in Karen's backyard, Joshua thought he saw the stars flick left, then right, as his upper eyelid fluttered. Karen shone her flashlight on a large circular star locator. She turned an outer ring to align the date and time of evening, studied the chart, then looked up at the sky.

"OK," she said. "Over there's Cassiopeia. It looks like the Little Dipper—you know, Ursa Minor?—but it isn't. Now let's see . . . There! Over there's the Little Dipper. OK, now see that last star in its handle? That's Polaris, the North Star. It's not quite true north, but it's close. Now just above that tree you can see the Big Dipper, right? And the two main stars of the Big Dipper point toward Polaris also. By the way, the Big Dipper is really a part of Ursa Major, the Great Bear. So it's actually a constellation within a constellation."

"Where did you learn all that stuff?" asked Joshua.

"Oh, I don't know. My father was interested in astronomy. He wanted to be an astronomer, but he ended up being a lawyer. He used to take me to the planetarium in New York, and got all these books, and— But that was back when he was still my father."

"Oh . . . Actually, of course, he's always your father, right?"

"No. Not if I don't want him to be."

"But I thought you said you were planning to visit him Saturday."

129

"I've changed my mind."

"Oh . . . Whatever you say. I understand."

"You do?"

"Sure."

"Thanks. . . ." She felt like hugging him for not questioning her. She moved closer to him on the blanket, and Joshua put his arm around her. She kissed him, quickly.

"OK, Josh, back to the stars, right? Don't answer. OK, now what I'd like to do is check out Polaris with your grandfather's compass. I've got it right here. Let's see if it points to the North Star."

She held the dime-sized compass out, and they both leaned over, heads touching, watching the needle turn and shimmer in moonlight. It swung past the North Star, then back again; its final position was slightly to the left of the star.

"Not bad, huh?" said Karen, tapping the compass and letting it seek north again. "It still works. Just think, your grandfather must have done this when he was our age. It almost gives you the chills. Like, when we're dead, someday someone will still be using this compass. Maybe I'll give it to my son or daughter, and they'll give it to theirs, and so on. . . ."

Joshua held her closer and kissed her on the side of her neck. "That's for while we're still alive," he said, and kissed her once more.

"Oh . . . I'm sensitive there. . . . Ohhh . . . the stars, Josh. Josh? The stars . . ."

It couldn't be resisted: the warmth, the ache, the wanting to hug, to kiss. They lay on the blanket, kissing mindlessly, eagerly, their legs pressing, entangled. Through clothing, Joshua could feel the smoothness and softness of Karen's body against his, moving, rubbing, holding, and—

It was going to happen if he didn't stop; he could feel it a moment away if he didn't stop pressing against her. He drew back and sat up abruptly.

"Karen, I—I better stop. . . . I've *got* to stop."

"But Josh—"

"Karen, it's too much! Now *I'm* saying it."

"Why? Is there something wrong?"

"No! It's just too much. I almost couldn't stop at all."

"Really?"

"Really."

"Oh, wow. . . ."

"Triple wow," said Joshua. "Next thing you know, I'll be saying, or you'll say, what do we need all our clothes on for? And before you know it, there we are."

"Right. Right . . . Oh, brother. . . . Maybe we need some more rules. Like—I don't know—Like nothing horizontal?"

"I guess so. . . ."

Karen laughed. "Pretty soon we'll have as many rules as the Supreme Court. . . . I hope my mother didn't look out the window before. Too bad she trusts me so much. I'm beginning to not trust myself. . . . Anyway . . . thanks, Josh."

131

"For what?"

"Oh . . . for being you. . . . Can I kiss you, politely?"

"Sure! Even impolitely!"

They kissed, a series of little pecks that grew into a long embrace, kneeling, facing each other. After a moment Karen drew back and looked directly at Joshua. "Oh, boy, Josh . . . I think we've got a monkey on our backs."

"I think you're right. So what do we do?"

"Follow our rules like crazy! Like right now, we go inside and eat some of my mother's fantastic homemade dansk kringle. . . . It's not fair! Teenagers can't win! We're damned if we do, and we're damned if we don't! I want to be twenty-one. Right now!"

"I'd settle for twenty," said Joshua with a snorting laugh.

As they sat in Karen's kitchen, Joshua felt his eyelid twitch badly. Well, now he had another reason for it. Comedians made jokes about things like this. Frustration. But it wasn't comical, at all; it was painful.

By Friday evening, Joshua had reviewed Valerian's most recent matches for the third time. It looked hopeless; there was no way he could ever beat Valerian. He'd be lucky to draw. It was almost ten P.M. when Karen phoned to tell him that Lori couldn't make it to New York after all. Joshua had half expected it.

"How come?" he asked, turning his stereo down.

"She says she has to go out to Long Island to her

132

aunt's. She forgot all about it, but her cousin is having a birthday party, and she has to go."

"You think she really does?"

"I don't know. She was just out there two weeks ago. . . . Josh, if she doesn't want to come with us, there's nothing we can do about it. But I believe her; she doesn't lie. . . . She's been pretty much out of it though, hasn't she?"

"I'll say. . . . You think she's OK?"

"Uh-huh. I think I have it figured out. Lori's a little sore, see, because she's actually afraid to go to a shrink, and I've pushed it into reality, talking to her mother. Her mother's still sore at me too, but I think she's thinking. I can tell. Yesterday she asked me on the phone, before she put Lori on, if I thought Lori was acting awfully quiet lately. And I said, 'Damn straight she is,' or words to that effect. I think I've gotten to her. What do you think, Josh? Mr. Psychologist?"

"I don't know. Could be."

"What time is our bus tomorrow?"

"Ten, on the nose."

"I'm still not watching your match, you know. I'm going downtown to pick up those posters for the anti-nuke rally. To which you're going to go, or I'll never speak to you again, right?"

"Right, right, right," he said.

"Good, good, good," she echoed.

"*Je puis, tu peux, il peut, elle peut, nous pouvons, vous pouvez, ils peuvent, elles peuvent.* How's that!" he asked.

133

"*Perdone, no hablo francés.*"

"*Je ne parle pas espagnol.*"

"*Adiós.*"

"*Au revoir.*"

"A kiss is coming through the phone to you," said Karen.

"The kiss is coming back," Joshua answered.

"God, what goo!" said Karen. "So long, Josh."

"So long, gooey." He felt a warm glow toward her, a flush of happiness, as if she were in the room with him.

If only Lori could be happy, too. So quiet all week. So withdrawn. And now not going with them to New York. If only, somehow, he could do something to make her happier. Anything. He pictured Lori's face, smiling, that evening before the dance.

Was it not having a boyfriend? Was that the problem? Probably. If only he could be two people at once, so he could go out with Lori, too. Not that he was so wonderful. But at least he was an improvement over Eric Glastonbury. If only—

18

Joshua hadn't been prepared for it; his table was surrounded by onlookers. All eyes were upon him at the start of his match with John Valerian. He was third coming into the final round, ahead of Benziger, Tellerman, and a dozen other first-rate players, and he was only fourteen. Well, almost fifteen, but the crowd didn't seem to care; he was their star for the day, the player to watch, as he sat opposite the United States chess champion.

Someone took flash pictures, and Edelbaum had to ask everyone to step back away from the table, to avoid a crush. They finally roped it off. His table, *his*! He wished Karen were there to see how important and exciting chess could be. But she'd gone downtown as

135

planned and wouldn't be back until three o'clock. By then the game might be over. By then he might well have lost.

Valerian had the white pieces; he chose the Giuoco Piano opening. Joshua couldn't believe it; Valerian had never used it in all the games he'd studied. The opening had gained some new interest since Karpov had tried it several times in the recent world championship match in Merano, Italy. But it was a draw opening; the game that developed normally was indeed *piano*: quiet, uneventful.

Joshua knew Valerian could win the tournament even if he lost this game; he was that far ahead. Most likely, he was aiming for a peaceful drawn game, unless Joshua made one of those small, fatal errors Valerian loved to exploit. At least he wasn't out to "kill" the teenager, but somehow the whole thing felt condescending to Joshua. A dumb, meaningless draw after all the flash photos and excitement.

Pawn to king four. Pawn to king four. . . . Knight to king bishop three. Knight to queen bishop three. . . . Bishop to bishop four. Bishop to bishop four. . . . Pawn to queen three. Knight to bishop three. . . . Knight to bishop three. Pawn to queen three. . . . It had become the *pianissimo* variation. The opening moves rolled on, symmetrical, peaceful, no thinking time needed. Book, all book.

Valerian moved his bishop to king knight five. Joshua answered with pawn to king rook three, chasing the bishop. Valerian shrugged and moved bishop to rook four. What! Why had he done that? He should have exchanged bishop for knight, which led to an approximately equal game. . . . Wait . . . wait . . . . A twist in the symmetry . . .

Joshua started sweating; the tension crept up his neck. He was shivering inside, yet sweating. Valerian, not he, had made that tiny error. A wasted move. A wrong approach. Joshua could exploit it. But how? By developing on the kingside, and hitting that bishop again with his king knight pawn. And castling queenside.

Joshua studied the board, his fingers gripping the edge of the table. The room disappeared as he followed, behind his eyes, five, six, seven moves deep. Pawn out. Valerian's bishop has to move. Then the queen into action. . . . Right, right. Try another variation, carefully, carefully. Another . . . another . . . OK.

Joshua moved his pawn to knight four. The crowd buzzed. Something was going on in the game. It was going to be a good one. The tempo was Joshua's now.

The minutes passed like hours. Joshua's eyes moved up and down the board, skinning it like a carcass, tearing out the entrails, pulling the position apart, putting it together. No blunders, please. No blunders. His eye twitched badly.

Valerian was concentrating. Brow knit now. Unlit cigarette between his fingers.

The game, the pieces, the board, became wet clay to mold, to form into a container of ideas and possibilities, into a vase reshaped again and again from the previous position. The twentieth move, the twenty-first, the twenty-second, and the momentum was still Joshua's.

The thirtieth move, the thirty-first . . . Still an edge. A slight edge, the pacing advantage, like the lead of a first violinist, making the music happen. Mozart. Chess was Mozart . . . .

Suddenly, from the corner of his eye or mind, Joshua saw it. From the corner of his thoughts, almost not recognized. It was there. A win. A forced mate.

If it were true, if it could happen, it would be incredible. A bishop sacrifice forcing a mate. Think it through, slowly. Slowly. All the time in the world. Think it through. Bishop takes pawn, check. Knight takes bishop. Queen to bishop four. . . . He can't do anything. He has to pull back the rook. He must. Then knight to bishop six, check. He has to move the king over. Wait. Wait. Then hit with the other knight. . . . It's forced. He'd won the game! He'd won it! . . . But wait. Patience. His grandfather's favorite word. Patience. Patience. Think it through again. Bishop takes pawn. Knight takes. Queen out. . . . If Valerian gave up his rook, he would still win it. Still forced. What if he sacrificed his queen, as a spoiler? Follow that variation. . . .

He noticed Karen in the crowd now, holding a roll of posters. She must have finished early; it was only two-thirty. Good! She would see this incredible match! . . . Now concentrate on that mate. Back to the variations. . . .

Five minutes passed. Valerian stood up and stretched.

138

He doesn't see it, thought Joshua. No one does. No one but me. It's got to be the trickiest mate in ten years. He can't do anything. I don't believe it! I want to scream! What a combination! . . . Go over it again. Again. Bishop takes pawn, check. If he moves the king, I still have it. Moves the rook. Still have it. Follow it again. Again. . . . Could Karen possibly know what's happening? No. Of course not.

Joshua stared at the board. There were eighteen minutes left on his chess clock. No rush. Think it through, nice and easy. . . . Or kick the habit?

That was crazy! Crazy! What a thought! Karen's mental telepathy! Kick the habit. Insane! Get back to the mating combination. . . .

But he could. He could do it. Theoretically. It would be absolutely insane. But it would cure him. Oh, would it! Forever. He'd never touch a chess set again. Very simple. Just don't move that bishop. Move a pawn instead. And draw.

Help people. . . . You'd play to be friends. . . . Stop thinking about that stuff!

His left eyelid twitched continuously. Sixteen minutes and thirty seconds left on his clock. The people watching the game were murmuring . . . .

"Please keep it quiet. Tournament in progress," Edelbaum called out.

He really could do it. And never play serious chess again. What did he need chess for? It didn't make anything in real life easier. Look at Valerian. He was divorced and his wife was suing him for child support.

Everyone knew it; gossip of the club. What kind of man wouldn't want to support his own children if he could? Valerian's generous gestures were only in the world of chess. The man was brilliant; he could have done anything! And here he was, losing a game against a snotty fourteen-year-old. Some life! . . . The same thing would be happening to him, Joshua, someday. Valerian. Klein. His grandfather. You become notations in a chess book. . . . Was it worth it?

Quit. Quit now. For Karen. For his mother and father. For everybody. Even for himself. Help people. Help Lori. . . . She seemed unhappy all week. So quiet and sad-looking.

Fourteen minutes left on the clock.

I'm in a chess match. Think! Bishop takes pawn—I've taken Lori's friend away from her. But we're willing to go out with her; she doesn't seem to want to go out with *us*. If only I could help her. If only Bob Kim was still here, and she liked him and he liked her. We could have been double-dating. If I could *be* Bob Kim by magic, and yet be myself at the same time . . . Didn't I think something like that last night? Crazy thoughts! Get back to the game! . . .

Take a draw. Screw chess! Take the draw. Too many other things. Take the draw and get out. If you win with a mate like this, against the U.S. champion, you'll never escape from it. They'll keep you there like a prize poodle. You'll be hooked forever. Get out now!

Twelve minutes left on the clock.

Think chess! This is crazy! Think chess! . . . The mate

140

would be beautiful. He still doesn't see it. I know the combination, so it looks easy. Like one of those puzzles. It always looks easy later. . . . Beautiful. Chess can be beautiful . . . like art . . . like Lori's pictures. . . . The same . . . the same. . . .

Eleven minutes, thirty seconds . . . .

Joshua's face was covered with sweat and he kept blinking his left eye. Karen wondered if he was sick. He looked dazed, just as Lori did sometimes. Not angry or aggressive now, but dazed. Spaced out. Was he on some kind of drug or medication? He looked completely out of it. Why was everybody whispering to each other? What was wrong? she wondered.

Joshua moved his hand toward the board, then pulled back. Valerian shrugged and shook his head as if to say, I don't understand. The chess clocks showed only nine minutes left for Joshua, but twenty-three minutes left for Valerian . . . . What was wrong?

Joshua looked at Karen. She felt slightly ill; he seemed so troubled. He must have a lost game. He must. Was it her fault, somehow? Should she have kept her mouth shut? . . . Well, if he lost, maybe it would be for the best. In the long run. For his whole life . . . .

Again, Joshua stared at the board. He rubbed his face; the sweat smeared his cheek. He seemed to be almost asleep; his eyes were shut tight in concentration.

His clock showed six and a half minutes left.

He opened his eyes and looked at Karen again. She smiled toward him and waved the cylinder of posters she was holding. Why was he almost in tears?

141

He reached out toward the board, hesitated for a moment, then moved bishop takes pawn, called *check*, and hit his clock.

There was an audible gasp from the crowd. "Blunder," a man standing beside Karen murmured. "He'll lose his damned bishop."

Valerian studied the board for three, four, five minutes. Again and again he shook his head. He hadn't seen it yet. It was hidden. It was delicate. But Valerian's long delay was a compliment to Joshua. It meant that Valerian respected him and was searching for the reason Joshua had thought so long, and had made this strange move. After six minutes, Valerian shrugged and took the bishop with his knight. Instantly, Joshua moved queen to bishop four.

Valerian looked at the move and studied it for a minute. He looked around at the crowd, then studied it again. He leaned back in his chair. He'd seen it now. He started nodding at Joshua. Then he pulled his rook back. Joshua, immediately, moved knight to bishop six and called *check*.

Valerian's hand was out toward Joshua. "Resign! . . . Brilliant!" he said. "The finest mating combination I've ever played against! Brilliant! Brilliant!"

Within seconds they were all over the board, the competitors, the onlookers, the chess columnists, playing out the mating combination, playing the alternatives, checking for all possible loopholes. There were none. It was absolutely airtight. Perfect. He had found a remarkable forced mate in six moves.

142

There was another round of flash shots as reporters and columnists for the chess journals and newspapers crowded around Joshua, flooding him with questions. He gave them some quick yes-no answers as he signed his score sheet and handed it to Edelbaum, then walked through the crowd toward Karen. She waved her rolled-up posters again.

"Hi!" she said. "Is everything OK?"

"You won't like it," he answered. "Because I won."

"It's all right; don't worry about it. It sounds like it was something terrific!"

"Maybe. I've ended up tied for second place in the tournament. And I just beat the U.S. champion. . . ."

"That's wild! OK! Let's celebrate! I can give you a hard time about chess tomorrow. But today, let's celebrate."

19

Lori had bought the flowers that Saturday morning. But why so many? She didn't know. Daisies, tulips, daffodils, peonies, irises, azaleas. She'd carried the enormous bouquet home on her bike. The perfume had suddenly filled her room, like mist, as she'd put the bouquet in a large ceramic pot and placed it by the window. Would the flowers turn toward the sun?

They had all gone out, her father, her mother, her sister; gone out shopping at the Lake Hills mall. To shop for what? For things. Things with batteries in them. With knobs. With buttons. Nice things. Nicer things. Nicest things. Thing things.

Everyone was gone. Karen and Joshua were in New York and the world was empty, empty, as empty as the

144

large ceramic pot had been before she'd filled it with flowers. As the room had been.

The flowers made a little world of their own by the window, a world of smells and colors and silence. They were her mute friends in the room; when she looked toward them, they knew it. She took a flower from the massive bouquet, a tulip, and played her fingers over it, feeling the petals yield and press back, like a small child whose head is stroked.

She placed the tulip on the floor outside her bedroom door, then took more flowers from the ceramic pot and placed them around the room, one by one. Placed them on her bed, her bureau, on the chair by the window, above the mirror, on the desk, the rug, the lamp, the sewing machine by the door.

Then she went to the bathroom and filled a glass with water, took out a bottle of pills marked: *One or two before bedtime for sleep. Mrs. Lindstrom. Dr. Gaines*, and went back to her room. For sleep. That would be nice. Blue-green sleep.

She lay on her bed and took a pill with some water and tried to let the blue-green happen. . . . She stood again, and took more flowers from the ceramic pot, took all the flowers and placed them everywhere, some inside her dress close to her body, and took another pill and some water and lay down and let the trees come over her head, let the grass come under her feet, let it all surround her. Let Karen and Joshua call from a distance, *Lori!* Let them run toward her, and took another pill, and the grass was fragrant now, new mown, flowers everywhere, and another pill, and now they could be alone together, all three, and another pill, alone together, no more hurt, no more crying, flowers, only flowers, and another pill, together the three of them forever, and another pill, and another, and another, and everything was blue, green, everywhere flowers, everything turning, Joshua, Karen, it was going to be good, it was going to be . . . Oh, everything together . . . and Joshua . . . it was . . . and it was . . . and Karen . . . and . . . it was . . . going to . . . be good . . . forever . . . and forever. . . . Easy . . . alone . . . together . . . going . . . to . . . be . . . going . . . good . . . be . . . going . . . it . . . was . . . it . . . was . . . was . . . was . . .

20

They sat at a table by the window. It had been Karen's idea, sandwiches and tea in an expensive coffee shop on Madison Avenue. As a minicelebration for Joshua.

"This is where my mother likes to go whenever we come in to the museums around here," she said. "I love it because you can sit and people watch. Like over there, Josh! See? There go some punk rockers! Purple Mohawk haircuts! Spaced *out*! They'd never be able to walk around Lake Hills, New Jersey, like that. People would laugh them right off the street. But that's what I love about New York. Right?"

"I don't know," said Joshua. "The thing I like best about New York is the great pastrami sandwiches and the Chinese food."

147

"You're kidding!"

"Now you know the real me," he said.

"Then why did you get a chicken salad sandwich here?"

"Because they don't have pastrami on rye. This place is too fancy. Next time we come in, I'll show you the best place in New York City for pastrami. Their sandwiches are two inches thick."

"Oh, gross. . . . Hey, Josh! Do you want to see one of these nuclear rally posters? I got ten of them! They were almost out of them, even though the rally is still three weeks away. I had to beg. Literally. But they are gorgeous! Look at this."

She unrolled the cylinder of posters. A row of bombs transitioned into a row of people with upraised arms. Above and below were the words: *Arms Race? Or Human Race?*

"Neat, huh?" she said, as she rolled up the posters again. "Lori said, last week, that she's going to paint three placards for us to carry at the rally. These posters are just for putting up around our area. I think we should have at least two at the school. Maybe three. And one at the supermarket. Let me see . . ."

"How about at the mall?" asked Joshua.

"Hey, good! Are we allowed to? Who cares! As good as done! Maybe Lori will come with us Monday and help put them up."

"But she doesn't seem to want to do anything with us at all anymore," said Joshua.

"Oh, that's just this week. She'll come with us. I've

148

been through her ups and downs a million times. You'll see."

"I hope you're right. . . . I really like Lori a lot. I really do. I like her an awful lot."

"I know. So do I." Karen studied Joshua for a second. "Maybe we could even start putting up some posters tomorrow. . . ."

"OK. That's great. OK."

Karen played with her sandwich, then studied Joshua again. "What . . . what do you mean, you really like her a lot; you like her an awful lot? That's a lot of likes. Do you mean you . . . you sort of want to go out with her?"

"I'm going out with *you*. But . . . I don't know. I wish I could, in a way, because—"

"You wish you could? You *can*! And she won't bug you about chess, either!"

"No! I mean— It's just that I feel—I don't know *what* I mean."

"You're great at saying I don't know! You're a champion at I don't know!" His face looked guilty! He did like Lori! *That* way! He did! Was it happening again? Like with Mark? Like with her father? Yes!

"Karen, come on! It's you I want to go out with! It's you I'm *going* out with! I didn't explain it right. Let me talk—"

"You don't have to talk! I can *see* it! I've just decided! I *am* going to visit my father! He lives right near here, and I'll see you in school Monday! So long!"

"Karen, wait! Please!"

149

She stood up so abruptly that her chair fell over. Grabbing her cylinder of posters, she tried to straighten her chair, then hurled it under the table and raced out of the coffee shop.

Joshua fumbled in his pocket for some money to pay the bill. His mind felt on fire. Could she be right! Did he actually want to go out with Lori? Was he hiding it from himself? Hadn't it passed through his mind twice in the last few days?

He tossed ten dollars on the table and ran after her.

As Karen half walked, half ran along Madison Avenue, she tried not to think. If she thought, she might panic. Or was she panicking already? . . . What a kick in the head! I don't know, but maybe I'd like to go out with your best friend, but I'm not sure, maybe, who knows, I like her a lot. That stupid jerk!

She looked back for a second. He was trying to catch up with her, dodging through crosstown traffic a block behind. Even from that distance she could tell that he looked miserable. For a moment she felt like stopping and turning—but no!

She started running. Her father's apartment, was it Seventy-third or Seventy-fourth Street? . . . That stupid, stupid jerk! What did he expect her to say? Oh yes, go ahead, go with Lori and make out with her, and I'll wait back at the ranch? Or you can go out with both of us! Me Monday. Lori Tuesday. How nice for him! . . . If she were a saint, maybe she'd say yes. It might be good for Lori. It might.

There was the apartment house. Big modern piece

of shit! Oh, no! Joshua was running now too. He even *ran* like a jerk! . . . Nuts! The doorman had to let her in; it would take forever!

She rushed into the outer lobby and called to the doorman, breathlessly, "Apartment 8B. Hiler-Lastman. Tell them it's Karen Hiler. Hurry, please!"

As the doorman reached for his intercom phone, Joshua entered the lobby.

"Karen! Please! Let me talk to you for a minute!" Everything was messed up now! Everything! Even in his confusion, he saw how much he loved Karen. Wanted her, needed her. He felt sorry for Lori, that was it. Sorry enough to wish he could become the boyfriend he thought she wanted, if he could be in two places at once. But he had said it to Karen so clumsily. He hadn't really said it at all. She wouldn't give him a chance!

"Josh, it's all right! I'm OK!" said Karen. "If you like Lori, *I* like Lori, and maybe it's good for everybody, OK? Big-hearted Karen has spoken! Now leave me alone!"

"But it's you! Karen, it's you! I—I need you! What I said was dumb! You didn't let me finish!"

"I'll talk to you Monday, OK? So long!"

"But you're sore! Please! Wait!"

She rushed through the lobby door to the elevator. As she looked back, she could see that the doorman was preventing Joshua from entering the building.

"Karen!" he called.

As the elevator door slid shut, she gestured toward him with a pushing motion of her rolled-up posters, as

151

if to say: Go home! He looked defeated. For a moment she thought of going back down to him. No! He had to figure it out himself. Maybe what he'd said was dumb, but he'd *said* it! And *looked* it!

At the door to her father's apartment, she pressed the buzzer and closed her eyes for a second. Please don't let me cry, and please don't let me insult Diane if she's there, too, which I pray she's not.

Her father stood at the open door, Diane just behind him. Both he and Diane looked bewildered, as if they'd been caught trespassing on someone else's territory.

"Hi," said Karen, sullenly.

"Karen, sweetheart," her father said. "What a wonderful surprise. God, I'm glad to see you. What a beautiful, beautiful surprise."

"Hello, Karen," said Diane, "I—I have a lot of shopping—all kinds of junk I have to return. You know how it is. You buy more than you keep . . . and I'm on my way out, so you and your father can have some time—"

"Thanks," said Karen, "but I'm just trying to get away from somebody and this was all I could think of. I'll be going in a minute."

"You what? . . ." Her father looked suddenly beaten.

Karen sighed. Don't hurt him. Don't. She was hurting enough for both.

"Oh, I . . . Oh, shit, Dad! I didn't mean that. I've just had this big fight that's all. With a boy. . . . I've been wanting to visit you—but—but I've had this big—

152

Oh, Dad! Nothing good ever happens to me! I feel rotten! Really *rotten!*"

She let him hold her, biting her lip hard to feel pain there, rather than inside. She was *not* going to cry. Not here. . . . So many years he'd held her like this when she was feeling miserable. So many. His smell of pipe tobacco, that same smell. His hand rubbing her back. . . . She tried to hold back the tears, but her face collapsed into a broken sob. Her posters fell to the floor.

She wept as he held her, as he walked her gently to the living-room couch, wept without thinking, convulsively, choking, spitting, helpless as a small child. Diane sat quietly in the kitchen, not knowing whether she should stay or leave.

"Oh, baby, baby, I'm sorry you've been hurt," her father said. "Oh, baby, I'm sorry. Oh, baby, I'm sorry. . . ."

As Karen's sobs finally subsided, Diane gestured to Karen's father that she was going out. He waved to her to stay. She pointed toward herself with emphasis, as if asking: Me? Are you sure? He nodded back, and she returned to the kitchen.

"Feeling a little better, sweetie?"

"Yes. . . . Please . . . call me Karen, Dad . . . please."

"OK. Karen. . . . This boy. Can I help you with . . . with your problem?"

"No . . . . I need some tissues. . . ."

153

"You like him, right?" he asked as he handed her a tissue box.

"Yes. I don't want to talk about it! I don't! I can handle it. I'm OK now. I am."

"OK. . . . How's everything else? How's school?"

"OK, I guess."

"Good. And how's your friend Lori?"

"She's OK. More or less."

"Mom?"

"Come on, Dad. You talk to her on the phone all the time."

"But maybe she doesn't tell me everything. . . . How is she, Karen?"

"What do *you* care?"

"Oh, Karen, for God's sake, I *care.*"

"Oh, bullshit!" She sat up straight, at the edge of tears, again.

Her father sat, silently, his right hand busily twisting threads on the sofa. Diane walked into the living room, gingerly, reluctantly.

"Karen," she said very softly, "would you let me talk—"

"No!"

"Please. . . . It won't take long, Karen. Please?"

"What?"

"I know you hate me," said Diane. "I don't blame you. I really don't. If you hate me, you hate me. . . . But don't hate your father. . . . He cares about your mother very, very much. He does, Karen. And he loves you very— Oh!" Her voice suddenly broke.

154

There was a long silence. "OK . . . I heard you . . ." said Karen finally.

"Thank you," Diane answered in a tiny voice.

After a long pause, Karen said, "I don't hate anybody. . . ."

"Thank you," Diane said again. "Thank you."

After another pause, Karen continued, "I guess I've been a bitch myself, right?"

"No!" her father called out.

"Oh yes I have. . . ."

"Never!" her father said. "You've been hurt badly, that's all it is. I almost didn't go through with this because of you. . . . Karen, I'll never be able to explain it to you. It happens. You fall in love. When you least expect it. It tears you to pieces. To ribbons. . . . I'll never be able to explain it. . . ."

"You just did."

"Well . . . you have to go through it to understand. . . ."

"I understand, Dad . . . I do . . . I think. . . ."

All three sat silently, trying to absorb what had happened, the realignment of feelings. Karen's father kissed her gently on the forehead.

"You always used to do that," said Karen.

"I've been wanting to do that again for a long time," he said.

"So have I," said Karen.

"Karen . . . you do know I love you. You *must* know it. . . ."

"I guess . . . OK, Dad! You're only going to hear

this once, so get ready! I'm going to the door now, because I want to get back to Jersey. Here goes. Ready? Listen."

"But we could all go out for dinner," her father protested as she picked up her roll of posters.

"I don't feel that good," said Karen. "Next time, OK? . . . Ready? Listen. One, two, three! I-love-you-too. So long."

She was out the door and on the way to the elevator before he could speak, but his face looking down the hallway was luminous.

21

Joshua tried to call Karen Saturday night. Her mother answered the phone.

"Oh, I'm sorry; she went to bed. She said she had a bad headache."

His headache, no doubt, because he'd caused it. It felt like an accusation delivered by proxy. If only Karen would let him talk!

"Oh . . . well, uh, could you tell her I called if she wakes up?"

"Certainly. . . . Joshua? I'm sure things will be all right," Karen's mother said gently.

The words were an unexpected gift. But Karen's mother was always nice. Was she merely being polite? Probably.

157

"Well, we . . ." Joshua hesitated. "We had a—a problem. She—I . . . Uh, please tell her I called. Please?"

"Of course, I will. Certainly."

"Thank you. Thanks a lot."

"Don't be too, oh . . . unhappy," said Karen's mother. "It will be all right. You're too nice for it not to be all right. . . . Good night now."

"Good night, Mrs. Hiler."

They must have talked, she and Karen. She knew something that Karen had told her about him, otherwise why was she being this up about things? Just from knowing him? But she didn't really know him. If she knew him, she wouldn't think he was nice, because he wasn't! He was a clumsy slob who created more problems than he solved! Who created problems every time he breathed.

He sat at the upstairs phone, wondering if he should go to sleep himself. He was feeling the strain of the week: the tournament, his parents, the schoolwork, Karen. Most certainly Karen. And even Lori's silence. . . . Maybe he could try calling Lori. Maybe Karen had spoken to her. Would that be too crazy, calling her? Just to see what was happening? He wouldn't say much, just sort of let her talk. . . .

He'd never called Lori before; he searched for her number in the phone book. Evan Lindstrom. Her father. Right.

Joshua hung up on the sixth ring; no one was home. They were probably still at her aunt's on Long Island. Just as well. He wouldn't have known what to say or ask, anyway. He never seemed to know what to do, except behind a chessboard.

He went to bed with his clothes on, kicking off his shoes, burying his head in the pillow. Slob, weirdo, clumsy jerk! He'd done it! A few stupid words and he'd messed up everything, *everything* with Karen. Hopeless! Hopeless! . . . But if she wouldn't even let him explain, maybe she was just as stupid and hopeless as he was. Maybe they were *both* idiots. For all her common sense, maybe she had a couple of bolts loose too, just as he did. The way she'd run out of that coffee shop was plain kooky. And suddenly visiting her father, after she'd said she felt she no longer had a father. Yes, she had a few bolts loose, too. Good . . . . The thought was strangely comforting to him, and helped ease him into sleep.

He awoke Sunday morning and was shocked to see that it was almost ten-thirty. How could he have slept this long? Twelve, no, thirteen hours! Could he call Karen at ten-thirty on a Sunday? It seemed late enough. Well, he'd wait till eleven. Was he afraid to call? Maybe, but eleven was it! Not one second later.

His parents were both in the living room. Why did they have that nutty look on their faces? They looked pleased, he could tell, but they were trying hard to not show it.

"Joshua, there's something in the papers," his father said, struggling to look disinterested. "Maybe you ought to read it."

It was the Sunday *New York Times*. Page one. A

159

small box in the lower left-hand corner was continued in the sports section. The headline read: PRIZE FOR BEST GAME TO TEENAGER. And the subhead: JOSHUA FREEMAN, FOURTEEN, SCORES AGAINST U.S. CHESS CHAMPION.

Joshua scanned the article rapidly: Impressive win against United States champion, New Jersey student, only fourteen, second in tournament at Metropolitan Chess Club, prize for best game, player to watch, grandfather was a grandmaster in his day. . . . At the end of the article the winning position was shown, and the entire game was listed in chess notation.

In a small way he was actually famous, at least to people who cared about chess. Had this happened to Benziger, he would have been green, purple, and yellow with envy. Yet all he felt was a dull emptiness. Karen's face, her angry exit from the coffee shop, her mother's words on the phone, kept circling in his thoughts. Had Karen seen the newspaper? Would she call about it, possibly as a way to make up? If only she would.

"Could you clip out the article for me?" asked Joshua.

"Articles! Plural!" said his mother. "Dad went out and bought three more copies of the paper."

"Of course I did. It's not every day . . ." his father said. "Look, whatever we've argued about, nobody can take this away from you. It's quite an achievement. Quite an achievement. *The New York Times* is nothing to sneeze at, right, Sylvia? If they say you're good, then you're good."

"They said Granpa was good too," Joshua answered quietly.

160

"Good or not, it's quite an achievement," his father repeated. "Can a father congratulate his son? Congratulations, Joshua. Put it there!" He shook Joshua's hand vigorously.

"All well and good," his mother said. "Congratulations, of course. But I warn you, Joshy—I mean *Joshua*! Don't let this go to your head too much. It's nice; it's wonderful; if I know your father, he'll put this article up in the furniture showroom, *but*—don't start getting funny ideas, Joshua. That's all. Enough said. Granpa won prizes, too. Enough said."

"*Thanks*, Mom!" said Joshua.

"That mouth, again! I think I'm going to start keeping score."

"I just said thanks."

"It's the *way* you said it."

The phone rang. As Joshua's mother picked up the receiver, she repeated, "It's the way you talk. Sarcastic. . . ." Then into the phone, "Hello. Yes . . . hold on just a minute." She held her hand over the phone and turned to Joshua. "It's for you. Karen. I'll bet you don't talk to *her* like that."

"Karen! Karen!" He raced to the phone. "Hi—hello. Karen?"

"Josh! Lori took some pills! I'm at Morristown Memorial Hospital. Can you get down here? Could someone drive you down?"

"What! What happened?" He felt his body go cold all over.

"She took sleeping pills. A lot of them. They found

161

her last night and . . . Her mother just called me this morning. They're still watching her. I'm scared! We shouldn't have gone into New York."

"OK, I'm on my way. It might take me half an hour."

"Oh, Josh, I'm really scared!"

"OK. OK. Take it easy, Karen. Stop taking all the blame. Just—please. Take it easy. OK?"

"OK. . . ."

"That's better. I'm on my way. So long." He hung up and turned to his parents. "Mom! Dad! Please! Drive me to Morristown Memorial. Now! Please! It's Lori!"

"What happened?" asked his mother.

"She's sick! She's sick! I don't know! Get me there! Please! Just get me there!"

"All right! All right! Let me get dressed," his father said.

"Dad, please! Hurry up! Please!"

The car sped down Route 287. His father, who never went over the speed limit, was doing seventy miles an hour. . . . Let her be OK. Let her be OK. Please. . . .

The hospital lobby; the elevator; the fifth floor. It was all a blur. Why did he feel so cold? The hallway was light green. All a blur. He'd asked his father to wait down in the lobby, but now he wished he had come up with him. This was the room. 537. . . . Please!

A doctor was talking to Lori's parents just inside the door to the room; he was busily explaining something. Joshua could see Karen in the room, bending over Lori's bed. He nodded to Lori's parents and slipped past them.

162

"I'm still here," Karen said loudly to Lori. "It's me, Karen, and I'm right here."

Lori answered, with her mouth open, "Karen . . . I'm here too. . . ." There was a tube attached to her arm and a bottle high on a stand. Joshua swallowed hard. Lori's face looked so small and pale; her lips seemed dry and slightly swollen.

"Josh is here, Lori!" Karen said, again speaking loudly and clearly. Then she said softly, to Joshua, "I think she's OK. . . ."

"Hi . . . Josh . . ." Lori said through her open mouth.

"Hi, Lori! Hi!" Joshua answered, trying desperately to sound cheerful. He took Lori's hand and squeezed gently. "Hey, Lori, come on. . . . We've got posters to put up—did Karen tell you?"

"Uh-huh." Lori nodded her head, slightly.

Karen gestured to Joshua to come over to a far corner of the room. "Lori," she said, "I'll be back in one minute flat! OK?"

As they stood by the corner window, she whispered to Joshua, "I didn't mean to panic, but she looked so bad, before. She's coming out of it pretty well, the doctor said. She may be able to come home in a day or so. He said she's really going to need therapy though. A lot."

"Do they believe it now, her parents?"

"Oh, God, yes!"

"That's good. That's one good thing from this. . . . Karen, are *you* OK?"

"I guess. . . ."

"Karen, I'm sorry about yesterday. I didn't explain things right—"

"I don't want to talk about that *now*!" Karen whispered back. "Not with Lori like this."

"But the doctor's just gone over to her. Can I talk for a minute, till he's done?"

"OK. What?"

"Well . . . what I said about liking Lori doesn't mean I don't like *you*. But I feel sorry for her and— Can she hear us?"

"No. But keep your voice low, anyway."

"She seems so unhappy and out of it that when she *is* up, it makes me feel up, too."

"Me too," said Karen.

"I do like her, OK? I wish I could help her and make her feel good. Like at the dance, before you came? For a couple of minutes, I swear, I think she was making believe I was her boyfriend a little. And she seemed happy. Not that I'm that great. It's just . . . That's all I meant, yesterday. I wish I could, you know, be twins if that would help her. I tried to explain, but it came out all garbage. And you didn't give me a chance. . . . Karen, I really, really like you. I do. You know I do. Please don't quit on me. . . ."

"Oh, Josh! You idiot! Don't you think I like you too? Why would I get that bothered if I didn't?" She could see she'd been wrong about him. Almost wrongheaded. Stubborn, just as she'd been with her father. Only Joshua hadn't deserved it at all.

"But—are we OK?" asked Joshua. "Is it peace?"

164

"Sure," said Karen. "Can't you tell?" She smiled, and Joshua felt his body lighten, as if he'd been released from chains.

As they stood by Lori's bed again, Karen stroked Lori's hand gently.

"Thank you, you guys . . . for coming . . . to see me," said Lori, speaking more coherently now.

"Oh, Lori," said Karen, "we're your friends. Where *else* would we be?"

Without thinking, Joshua bent over and kissed Lori on her cheek, turned and surprised Karen with a sudden kiss on her lips, then kissed Lori on her cheek again.

"Come here, idiot!" Karen put her arm around Joshua and tried to hug both him and Lori at the same time. They ended in a sprawl on the bed. "Lori, are we crushing you?" she asked.

"No," said Lori. "I like it! . . . But that tube is . . . pulling. . . ."

Lori's mother turned and saw Joshua and Karen half on the bed, their arms around Lori. "What are they *doing*! What's wrong!" she called out. Lori's father looked apprehensive too. The doctor laughed and said a single laconic word to Lori's parents: "Therapy." Then he ushered her parents into the hall.

"We love you, Lori," said Karen, suddenly sitting up, serious. "We do! But if you ever try what you did again, I swear I'm not going to come around. Right, Josh?"

"Right," Joshua said. But why *had* Lori done it? he wondered. Why?

165

"OK, Lori! Don't say your best friends didn't tell you!" said Karen.

"Uh-huh . . ." Lori murmured.

"Because they just did!"

But something was still wrong, Joshua felt, in spite of the surge of good feeling. Even though things seemed so much better with Karen, even though Lori was OK, something was wrong beneath the surface of their friendship. He could sense it, as he could a chess game that was in trouble. Yet he couldn't say what it really was. Not yet.

22

Joshua's grandfather called Sunday afternoon and told him the forced mate was nothing new. He'd seen it used in Geneva in 1928 . . . but never mind. Never mind. It was beautiful chess. A piece of poetry. A ballet. Still, he'd beat the pants off Joshua on his next visit. An hour later Bob Kim called from California; the match had been reported in *The Los Angeles Times*. His congratulations were warm and generous, without any hint of envy. If only a continent didn't separate them. Maybe someday . . .

Joshua tried to force his way through his homework, but his mind kept drifting away from the history book back to Lori. To all three of them. He lay full length on his bed trying to think, trying to sort out all that had

167

happened in the past four days. But it wasn't like chess; there were bits and pieces of feelings and events that he couldn't fit together into any smooth arrangement.

Maybe he'd try to talk to Karen about it later. She was still at the hospital with Lori. It had all seemed so simple a few days ago: Karen and Lori, friends, a girl friend, milk shakes and pizzas and kissing in the movies. But now . . . what if Lori really tried to do something like that again? Who could ever stop it? At least she was going to get help now, real help instead of his and Karen's stupid ideas, like that dance.

She must have taken those pills while he was playing chess. While his chess clock was running, Lori had tried to stop all the clocks of her life, forever.

Maybe Karen was more right about chess than he'd like to admit. It couldn't help Lori. It hadn't even helped *him*. What good was it? No doubt he'd obtained his master's rating with second place in the tournament, and his name had been in a few newspapers. But he was still the same Joshua Freeman he'd been last week, with socks that didn't fit right, with bony elbows and knees, and a brain above average in nothing but chess maneuvers. He'd wanted chess to make him powerful, manly, graceful; to raise him up like Mozart, towering over others, so that he could be admired and have friends and be all good things forever. He'd been Mozart all right, with that great mating combination. He'd been Mozart for five minutes, but he would still be Joshua Freeman for the rest of his life. No one but Mozart could be Mozart.

168

The only friend he'd ever made through chess had been Bob Kim, and even that had been a lucky chance. Karen hated his chess playing, and Lori couldn't care less. Neither of them would ever understand that mating combination, and it didn't matter at all to them. What *did* they see in him? His falling socks? His bony, sloppy self? He saw so much in them; it was clear in them. Karen, like good earth, like dark bread. Lori, like slivers of light. They weren't champions at anything. They were just themselves, and it was enough; it was all that really mattered. Karen's decency. Her warm smile. Her good, generous eyes. Lori's giggle. Her sadness. Her sudden enthusiasms. But what could they see in him? His jerkiness? . . .

Yet they liked him. It was strange. The friendships had sprung from nowhere, from luck, from the juxtaposition of the sun, or moon, or stars, as it had with Bob Kim. Unexpected. The little lasso of *yes*, you're it, *yes*. We fit together, you and I.

There was a fit, a matching, a recognition somewhere. But what? . . . Maybe it was a secret knowledge that they weren't quite human, but freaks of another species, freaks who had to band together to survive. There weren't that many freaks to pick from; they were all in their own small packs, and that's why it was so hard to find friends. They were scattered over the earth, disguised as humans, hiding, fixing, hoping, going crazy. Hurting each other, even as they tried to avoid hurting. Even as they . . .

Suddenly he saw it, or thought he saw it, with the

169

corner of his mind, just as he'd seen that mating combination. Saw what was wrong. What was happening to them.

He went to his bookcase, searching among books titled *The Caro-Kann Defense*, *Endgame Strategy*, *Selected Chess Games of Mikhail Tal*, for his psychology paperbacks: *Elements of Psychology*, *The Psychology of the Adolescent*, *A Primer of Behavioral Psychology*. He pulled out the second book and flipped through the pages, stopping at the chapter entitled "Suicide."

At three A.M. he finally fell asleep, psychology books all over his bed.

23

Joshua, Karen, and Lori sat on the floor in Joshua's room Friday evening, while Mozart's music blossomed around them, creating a garden of pure sound. Every so often they dipped their hands into a huge bowl filled to the brim with popcorn.

Lori had come home from the hospital that Monday, and had gone back to school Wednesday afternoon. She'd started seeing a psychologist, and had had several intensive sessions those first few days. Yet Karen had felt that Lori was still holding back, was still withdrawn. She hadn't laughed once all week. What could they do? . . .

All that week neither Karen nor Joshua had mentioned the suicide attempt while with Lori. But it was

171

there, close to them, present in their very avoidance of the subject. It was even present in Karen's unrelenting cheerfulness. And when they were alone, Karen had told Joshua that she was afraid to go out just with him now; afraid to leave Lori behind. Joshua had expected it. It seemed to be part of what was wrong. Clearly wrong.

On Thursday Karen had suggested that they, all three, meet Friday evening to be together and relax and float in good feeling. And Joshua had immediately volunteered his house; his parents would be out.

The music from Joshua's stereo continued along its intricate course. Mozart was like a magician, always ready with one more trick, one more surprise. . . . Everything was smooth right now; Lori seemed the happiest she'd been all week. How could he talk to them? Joshua wondered. How could he tell them what he felt? And what if he were mistaken?

"I'm really beginning to get into this kind of music," said Karen. "You can almost *see* it. It's like a piece of embroidery."

"It's a million miles from Joni Mitchell," said Lori. "But I don't know, it reminds me of her, in a way, because it keeps changing and almost builds on itself."

"I like it a lot," said Joshua. "Mozart always reminds me of chess."

"Oh, right. Speaking of good old chess," said Karen, "now that you've been in the papers and everything, I guess I'm crazy to ask. But weren't you going to think about it all? Remember?"

172

"I did think about it," said Joshua. "And I've decided I won't quit."

"Oh." Karen looked hurt and troubled.

"I hope it doesn't make you sore," said Joshua. "But I've been thinking a lot about all three of us—"

"It's not going to make me sore!" Karen interrupted. "It's just that I think you're—you're *diminished* because of it. You could use your brains for so many good things. Instead, you're going to be out to win stupid chess games like any macho football player!"

Joshua stood up, went over to the stereo, and shut it off. A white silence filled the room.

"Don't fight, you guys," said Lori. "Come on!"

"I'm not fighting," said Joshua. "But I don't think we should sit around just listening to music, either. We're supposed to be friends, right? Well, if there's things wrong—and I think there are—then we should really talk. Remember, Karen? You're the one who said you believe in talking. Well, so do I."

"But you *have* talked!" said Karen. "You're going to be a macho chess player. That's it!"

"But that's not it! That's not it at all! It's your— things like your *I'm diminished* stuff. *That's* it. You're into all these causes, and that's great. But—but you can't turn me into *you*! I'm *me*! And if I look macho playing chess, then maybe just don't watch me play. You want to know what I think is wrong? We're trying to—to— How can I say it? We're trying to manipulate each other. All three of us. Me too. Lori too. We are!"

"Leave Lori out of this," said Karen, her face taut

173

with held-in anger. "It's between us. Leave her out of this!"

"No! I don't think we should treat Lori like a cripple. We've been treating her like a cripple all week. We'll end up doing it forever."

"Why are you picking on me?" said Lori. "I'm not doing anything to you!"

"Lori, I—I know you don't think you are," said Joshua. "But . . . do you know, Karen's afraid to go out with me now? She said so yesterday. She's afraid to go to a movie with me unless you come along too. . . . I like you, Lori, more than you'd ever think. I do. But—but I want to be alone with Karen sometimes. We have to be alone."

"I'm not stopping you!" said Lori. "Am I stopping you, Karen?"

"No, of course you—" Karen began.

"But Lori, you are," Joshua cut in. "Can't you see that you are? Don't you realize it? I don't know if I'm saying this right—"

"I'm not! . . . I feel bad sometimes, but it's got nothing to do with you. I have a right to feel bad sometimes."

"Josh, leave her alone!" Karen shouted.

"Lori, listen a minute. At that dance, remember? The second I put my arm around Karen, you were gone. And ended up getting drunk. And I felt sorry for you. We both did. . . . Then Karen and I go into New York together, and you end up taking an overdose of pills. And we felt sorry again—"

"I feel bad sometimes!"

"OK. Sure. I know you feel bad sometimes, Lori. Everybody feels bad sometimes. And you've probably got more problems than most—"

"I *do* have problems!" Lori pleaded.

"But what you're doing to us is a problem too," Joshua continued. "Underneath, I think you're sort of trying to make us feel guilty. I think you're angry at us. Can't you see that?"

"I am *not*! You're trying to make *me* feel rotten!"

"Enough, Josh!" said Karen. "Lay off!"

"Lori, I'm just trying to make you see what's going on. Underneath, not purposely. Subconsciously, or whatever the right word is. Underneath, Lori, I think you're trying to—well, to sort of hurt us with the drinking and the pills." Was he saying it right? Somehow, it was coming out clumsy. Heavy-handed. Blunt.

"I am not! You're wrong! I am not!" Lori shouted.

Joshua held his breath. Lori was angry now, and was beginning to show it. For the first time. If he was right, then that was good. It was in every book he'd read. Her kind of depression was repressed anger, he was almost certain. Anger held in, unrecognized, bottled up, turned back on herself instead of at them.

"Go on, Lori," said Joshua. "Tell me! Tell *her*!" He pointed toward Karen.

"You think I did that on purpose! I've got problems! Karen knows! Karen, tell him!"

"Josh, you can't treat us like one of your chess games!" said Karen. "Lori is a human being!"

"I'm—I'm saying this stuff for a reason, Karen! Give

me a chance! I've been reading psych books about this for five days now—"

"That's not enough!" Karen shouted. "You have to study it for years! —Oh, God, Lori, you must hate us both now!"

"OK! Good!" said Joshua. "Hate us, Lori! Go ahead! Even if it hurts. It's better than—than trying to kill yourself!" Too much! Too much! Why had he said it?

"You bastard!" Lori shouted.

"You're an amateur, Josh! Stop it! —Lori, I don't think you're trying to do things to us! I don't!"

"I'm not! I'm not! You two are doing things to *me*! All the time! I love you both, and you disappear! I— You kiss and hug and kiss and I want to be there! I want it to be *me*! With both of you! See? Josh? With *both* of you! With Karen too! Both!"

So that was it. . . . He'd been stupid. There were more problems than he'd realized. Karen was right. You have to study psychology for years! . . . His mind raced. Chess under pressure . . . What did he know about bisexual things? Didn't plenty of kids actually go through that kind of phase? Hadn't he even felt that way about Bob Kim once, himself, for a while? Yes, maybe, but it had passed, almost out of his memory. And for some people it wasn't just a phase. . . . Things were more complicated than he'd thought. How much of the pill taking had been repressed anger? How much her being troubled over her sexuality? Or other things? Lori probably couldn't say, herself. Yes, it needed slow, careful analysis. . . . Should he quit? But he was on a

176

track that seemed right, at least for part of the problem. Try to finish. Try to make it clear to Lori. But carefully. Carefully.

"OK," said Joshua. "I see what you're saying, Lori. I see. With both of us. . . . And it hurts, right? Right?"

Lori nodded, yes. Tears were flooding down her face.

"And you can't have what you want," Joshua continued. "And you—you think you can't tell us, or anybody, because nobody will ever accept you—"

"Because people are prejudiced!" Lori shouted through her tears.

"OK," said Joshua. "And you're actually angry, maybe, at the whole world, in a way, right? And it hurts. We go off, and we hurt you even more. And the worst is, you have to act as if you like us all the time, when sometimes you probably hate us both, because you're hurting a lot. Right, Lori?"

Her mouth was bubbling with tears, as she nodded her head up and down.

"You can't even say to yourself: 'I hate you. You're hurting me; I hate you at the same time that I love you.' So you do the sleeping pills thing. Now we can be sorry. Look what we made you do. . . . Lori, do you think, maybe, that's what it's all about? Or some of it, at least?"

She nodded again, her face a sea of tears.

"Lori, I like you," said Joshua. "I don't care if you're half gay, or half straight, or half *purple*! I like you exactly as you are. But I can be angry, too, when you put a weight like those pills on our backs. I need Karen.

177

I like her. I *love* her, I do, even though she's such a pain in the ass, sometimes. And you *are* a pain sometimes, Karen, with that chess stuff! You are! See, that's what's wrong with *me*! I've never said something like that. I guess I take all my frustration and aggression out in chess. See, Lori? That's what *I* need to do, too. To let myself feel what's inside, and get done with it, and not keep being such a wimp!"

"OK, Josh," said Karen. "You sit here on your royal throne, telling us where to get off! King Joshua, the only holder of divine wisdom!"

"I'm not on any throne," said Joshua. "Because I've done things to you, too, Karen. I have! I've been thinking plenty. But first . . . Lori, are you OK? Because what I've been saying . . . it was only so we could be, like, *real* friends. So you could talk to us and not hide things, and we could talk to you, too. Lori, please? Do you understand what I've been trying to do?"

She nodded once more as she tried to control her tears. Then in a broken voice she said, "I know— you're . . . you're not a—a rat, Josh. . . . I'm not . . . *that* stupid. . . ."

"Don't be so sure he's not a rat!" said Karen. "Maybe he is! What rat things have you been doing to *me*, Josh? Go ahead!"

"Come on, Karen," said Joshua. "OK, maybe I *am* a rat. I don't know what a rat is. All I know is, I've been afraid that if I didn't do what you wanted me to do—give up serious chess—I'd lose you. So I'll think about it, and I'll delay, and I'll do this and I'll do that,

178

even though I know damn well I'm not going to give up chess just because you say I should. But I've been afraid to tell you. To say: That's me! Take it or leave it! . . . I guess I did just now, though. Finally. . . . See? All three of us doing things to each other. Not because we're rats. Because we—we need each other. . . ."

They sat without speaking, trying to sort out their feelings. Could he be right, Karen wondered. About Lori? And about the chess? It made sense, what he'd said about Lori. Hadn't *she* felt Lori's resentment? *Are you going to go to bed with him?* Things like that. She had never wanted to believe that Lori could be other than perfect, other than loving. But if that was all she was, how could she really be human? And what about the chess business? Hadn't she tried to change Joshua into a version of herself, as he'd said? Instead of standing on her own two feet, being what *she* was, and letting him be what *he* was. . . . Wasn't that a feminist goal? Wasn't that what her mother was actually trying to do?

"I . . . I took a chance," said Joshua, finally. "That you could see this was meant to help. I guess I was wrong. . . . I guess I've screwed it all up."

Karen said very quietly, "Maybe you're not all that wrong. But you did it, that whole thing with Lori, so—so damn *sure* of yourself."

"OK," said Joshua. "You're probably right. . . . Next time I have some friends,—if I ever do—I'll do it better."

"You've got friends now," said Lori softly.

"Lori, do I?"

"Yes. . . ."

179

"Thank you, Lori. . . . I guess, maybe, I got carried away. . . ."

"No, my shrink's been—been fooling around with that stuff, too . . . that you said about me. It's . . . it's awful, because it makes me sound so *selfish*!"

"No!" said Joshua. "You *do* have problems, Lori."

"Lor, you look pretty terrible," said Karen. "Are you really all right?"

"I guess. . . . You know, I never called anybody a bastard before in my whole life. . . ."

"That's not going to fix everything," said Joshua. "All this anger stuff, maybe, is just the tip of the iceberg. There's probably a lot of things. The way the books describe it, it takes time. To, you know, figure out what's going on inside you, making you hurt yourself like you did. It can take months. Sometimes years. . . ."

"And you went ahead and tried to fix it all in ten seconds!" said Karen. "Lor, are you really sure you're OK?"

"Yeah. And I'm not even going to apologize for calling you a bastard, Josh."

"Good!" said Joshua. "I'm not going to apologize to Karen for calling her a pain."

"You don't have to," said Karen. "Sometimes I *am* a pain. I'm probably a pain for telling you *this*, too, but I think you lucked out, Josh! Because I think what you were doing, playing psychologist, was as dangerous as hell! And I'll bet Lori agrees!"

"I know," said Joshua. "But our friendship, all around,

180

was like—like a game of pretend. Now, at least, I think we're out in the open. All of us. . . ."

"OK, Josh!" said Karen. "You've trapped yourself! You just proved you should be doing psychology, not chess. Right?"

"You're doing it again," said Joshua. "Pain! Pain!"

"Don't . . . please don't fight anymore," said Lori. "Not even in fun."

"OK," said Joshua gently. "Hey . . . does anybody want to hear some Mozart now? . . . Lori? Karen? . . ."

As the music filled the room, swelling like a sail in a sudden breeze, Joshua sighed with relief. He had done it, and things seemed all right. Maybe Karen was right about doing psychology. Maybe he *had* proved something, after all. It had been frightening, that last half hour. His mind had raced as much as in any chess match; he was totally covered with sweat. But for the first time in his life, he sensed a glow of having done something difficult, something valuable, *not* behind a chessboard. Even if it had been clumsy. Even if he'd made plenty of mistakes.

24

It was a bright, clear day in June. They had come to New York by the tens of thousands, from Vermont and California, from England and Japan. The marchers filled the avenues and overflowed into every side street as they progressed past the United Nations buildings, chanting: *One, two, three, four! We don't want nuclear war!* The crowds, the children, the giving and taking of bread-cake-cheese-soda-wine, the floats, the enormous puppet figures towering over the marchers, the posters and banners and flags, created, for a few hours, a fiesta of peace, a carnival of hope.

Lori, Karen, and Joshua worked their way through the crowds, holding the placards Lori had painted. Under white doves against a blue background, the words *I*

Love Peace were emblazoned. They moved as best they could in the mob, past children with whitened faces wearing gas masks, past a Japanese group carrying a block-long linen scroll inscribed by thousands, past the gigantic figures of the Bread and Puppet Theatre. Karen had not been able to locate the Women for Women group from New Jersey; the side streets were so jammed that the meeting points had been altered.

"We should have come with my mother on the chartered bus!" Karen shouted over the blare of a nearby loudspeaker. "We're going to have to march on our own, you guys!"

"That's OK!" Lori called back to her. "So long as we're here!"

They moved with the crowds past the United Nations buildings, through an underpass onto Forty-second Street, then back up toward Central Park along Fifth Avenue. In the turmoil they met several students from their high school and one of Karen's neighbors who had moved to Massachusetts years ago. They embraced each time as if they'd met in a far country, sharing in a newly discovered community and closeness. Joshua had seen such moments only at family celebrations. But everyone seemed to feel like one family today, in the crush of goodwill.

They entered the park; there was room now to walk side by side. Joshua hesitated a moment, then put his free arm around Karen. Lori looked toward them; her smile was gone. She took a deep breath, as if she were fighting something within her, then called out, "Hey,

183

guys! Look! Up ahead! They've brought some of those huge puppets into the park!" She walked ahead a short distance, slipping by other marchers.

Karen put her free arm around Joshua, too, and they squeezed as they walked, their placards awry. "I don't know, Josh," she said. "I don't know. . . ."

"She's OK, Karen," said Joshua. "It's been three weeks now. She's handling it better and better."

"I guess I'm probably going to worry about her for the rest of my life."

"Karen, you can't! She's OK. And she'll find someone, too. She's too nice not to find someone." He suddenly realized he'd repeated the words Karen's mother had used about him, that Saturday evening on the phone.

"She's walking back," said Karen. "Maybe we ought to unhook, Josh." She tried to pull free, but Joshua still held her.

"Hey, they're doing a dance with those puppets, down around the bend! They're really skillful! . . . Why are you both looking at me like that?"

"Lori . . . you see how we're walking," said Karen. "Is it OK?"

"Of course!" She swallowed hard and made her face widen into a smile. "I'm great. Don't worry. . . ." She knew it would always hurt. Always. But they did love her, that was clear. Very few people had two friends who loved them. Who really loved them. It was good to be alive, to be here in this park, where everybody was everyone's brother or sister for a little while because of the day, and the bright sun, and the music, and the little kids, and peace. . . . But would she ever have someone all her own?

They came to a high hill overlooking the path of the marchers heading toward the expanse of the Great Lawn, toward the program of speakers and entertainers. Joshua suggested they climb up and rest awhile; they'd been walking now for over four hours. They could eat the cheese and apples and cake they'd brought with them.

From the top of the knoll, they could see the winding path with the mobs of oncoming people, back, back, out of sight, with their banners and signs in every color, size, and shape, proclaiming *Peace—No More Nukes—Save Our Children*. And out on Fifth Avenue, paralleling the park, other thousands marching, entering the park farther north.

"If only they'd do this all over the world," said Lori.

"They will. They will," said Karen. "There's been a lot of this in Europe already. . . . God, look at that mob out there! I wonder if it's going to be a million."

"I heard someone say that the news reported seven hundred thousand," said Joshua.

They ate their cheese and apples as they watched, almost hypnotically. The unending flood of men, women, and children would go on, it seemed, forever.

"Someday," said Karen, "I want to really work on things like this. You know what's wrong with us? We're all wrapped up in our own tiny little world. All we worry about is Do I like you, and Did you do this to me, and Are we mad at each other or glad at each other. But you see a thing like this, all these thousands of people

185

marching, and oh, wow! It lifts you right out of your skin. It does, as they say, permanent damage. You're never the same again. . . . I'll always be into causes, I guess. That's the only talent I've got. If that's a talent, which I doubt. . . . Not like being an artist like you, Lori, or a chess champion like you, Josh. Notice, Josh! Acceptance! My friend the chess champ!"

"I don't know," said Joshua. "I think you actually got to me, Karen. Finally. Maybe I'll do psychology, after all. Did I tell you? I've started reading more psych books. . . . Or maybe I'll do both. I want to sort of just let life happen for a while. Like being here, today. . . . I know one thing, I'm not studying chess stuff as much as before. I'd rather be doing things with you two."

"I know what I want to do," said Lori. "I like to draw and all that, but what I really want is to start a farm somewhere, with friends like you, and raise vegetables and things, and live off the land. A place where we could really be ourselves. And then, if the H-bomb fell, we would have been happy up till then, doing things, and being together. . . ."

"It sounds good," said Karen. "It sounds like a nice dream. . . ."

"I know it sounds like a fairy tale," said Lori. "But at least I'm telling you this, because I used to do nothing but daydream about this sort of thing. But even if it's just a dream, what's so wrong with wanting a place where everybody can be happy, and not hurt each other, and love each other? This march today was somebody's dream once, too."

186

"Oh, God, you're right, Lori," said Karen. "Lor, if you could only get it all together, you could do anything."

"I'm going to get it all together. Because that's what I want to do; I want to make it really happen, that farm. And anyone passing by will say: Look at that. Those people are so happy there. They made it all with their own hands. That big green barn and that fence and all those fields, way out there to the woods. . . . Do you think we could, you guys? Do you think we ever will?"

"Maybe I'm crazy," said Joshua. "But I think we've already begun."

"We could form a company," said Karen. "Weirdos Incorporated. Normals need not apply. Let's put it to the vote. All in favor say *aye*."

"Aye."

"Aye."

"Aye."

"Passed and carried," said Karen. "Now all we have to do is grow up . . . if they'll let us."